AMERICA FALLEN!

AMERICA FALLEN!

The Sequel to the European War

By

J. BERNARD WALKER

1915

PREFACE

THIS book has been written entirely without prejudice. What Germany did could be done by more than one of the great naval and military powers of Europe. That she has been chosen to point the moral of our unpreparedness is due to the fact that German unity of thought and action provide the strongest contrast to the lack of harmonious purpose and co-ordinated effort which characterize the United States.

J. B. W.

NEW YORK,
  April, 1915.

CONTENTS

CONTENTS

AMERICA FALLEN!

I

THE Treaty of Geneva, which brought to a close the European War, was signed, on March 1, 1916, by the peace plenipotentiaries of no less than thirteen nations.

Throughout the spring, summer, and winter of 1915, the titanic conflict, enlarged by the entry of over 3,000,000 troops of Italy and the Balkan States into the theater of operations, swayed to and fro across the blood-soaked soil of Europe, with a ferocity and slaughter which sickened even the most hardened veterans of the war. Weight of numbers and a crushing superiority in artillery drove the armies of the Dual Monarchy back upon Budapest and Vienna, held the redoubtable Von Hindenberg within his own frontiers, and rolled the German armies in France and Belgium slowly back to the Rhine and the Dutch frontier.

Undismayed, and fighting against heavy odds with a magnificent courage and steadiness, Germany took up a seemingly impregnable position on the right bank of the Rhine and marshaled her forces for a strictly defensive campaign in 1916. Late in November of 1915, however, when by common consent the warring hosts on the Western battle line had apparently settled down for comparative rest and recuperation during the winter months in a quasi-defensive, similar to that of 1915, Holland suddenly declaring war, entrenched herself heavily on the German border, and a vast Allied reserve army, entering Holland by the Belgian-Dutch border, and by way of Rotterdam and Amsterdam, concentrated to the east of the Rhine, drove down in a resistless offensive into Westphalia, taking the German army in the right flank and rear, and captured the great centers of artillery and ammunition supply in Essen and the surrounding districts.

Germany, realizing that, with the Krupp and other factories in the hands of the enemy, the war must end automatically, accepted the friendly offices of the Swiss Government and the peace conference opened at Geneva.

And thus it came about that there gathered on the shores of the placid lake the most momentous conclave in all the history of the world.

Contrary to universal expectation the deliberations moved forward with a swiftness which, considering the enormous interests at stake, appeared to a nervously apprehensive world simply incredible. And herein was seen the advantage, costly though it had been in blood and treasure,

of carrying the gigantic struggle through
to an absolutely decisive issue.

The earlier d͏ ͏erations, relative to the
readjustm͏   ͏oundaries and territory,
moved ͏apidly to their expected results.
Rus͏ ͏a, content with the possession of Con-
stantinople, and the extension of her frontier to the Carpathians, agreed readily to
the re-creation of Poland as an autonomous
and " buffer " state between herself and
Germany.   To Roumania was given
Transylvania on the condition, arranged
previously to her entrance into the war,
that she return to Bulgaria the territory
wrested from her during the second Balkan War, and Servia was enlarged by the
acquisition of Herzegovina and Bosnia.
The boundary between Italy and Austria
was rectified so as to restore to Italy her
lost provinces.   France, as the reward of
the heroic struggle of her citizen soldiery,
regained possession of Alsace and Lor-

raine. Japan was permitted to hold Kiao-
Chou and acquire from China the lease
formerly held by Germany, a pledge being
given for the maintenance ʿ the "Open
Door" in that country.

So far, so good; but when it c. me to
the insistence by the Allies on an inden..nity
of fifteen billion dollars, the first install-
ments of which were to be paid into the
Belgian treasury, Germany presented an
adamantine front. And to the demands
of Great Britain that the German fleet be
reduced by the distribution of its major
units among the fleets of the Allies, she
retorted that if the transfer of so much as
a ship's launch to a foreign flag were again
suggested, Germany would withdraw at
once from the convention, and "would
fight it out until the last mark, the last
loaf of bread, and the last man was
gone!"

The convention was adjourned for a

week; and in view of the uncompromising front presented by Germany and Great Britain, and the probability of a continuance of the war to the bitter end, the world was thrown into a state of profound despondency and foreboding.

The next session was marked by the most dramatic incident of the whole conference. No sooner had the meeting been declared open than the German plenipotentiary abruptly announced that he had received instructions from Berlin to state that, if no more mention were made of the dismemberment of her fleet, Germany would agree to pay an indemnity to the Allies of fifteen billion dollars, and give the customary pledges therefor.

The curt announcement of Germany's assumption of this stupendous obligation produced, even in that well-poised assembly, a barely-checked murmur of astonishment. The British plenipotentiary asked for a three days' adjournment. He was instructed by his home government to stand firm for the disruption of the German navy; but on his cabling that it was the unanimous opinion of the rest of the Allies, that the assumption by Germany of this enormous indebtedness would so far cripple her financially as to render any material increase of her naval forces impossible before the existing ships were becoming obsolete, he was instructed to accept the German conditions.

And so, on the 1st of March, 1916, the thirteen signatures which ended the greatest moral and material tragedy in the whole history of the world were appended and peace settled over the stricken people of Europe.

And, thereafter, men said to one another when they met: " How came it about that Germany so suddenly agreed to pay that fifteen-billion-dollar indemnity? "

II

THE COUNCIL CHAMBER AT POTSDAM

ON the morning of the day following the signing of the Peace of Geneva, Germany's plenipotentiary, Count Von Buelow, entered the Council Chamber at Potsdam punctually at the hour appointed. There was gloom upon his face—and weariness, too; for throughout the night journey to Berlin, the burden of that fifteen-billion-dollar indemnity, which the Kaiser had authorized him to impose upon stricken Germany, had lain heavily upon his mind. Heavy gloom sat also upon the faces of the distinguished company around the council board. Von Hollweg, the Imperial Chancellor was there, and the foreign secretary, Von Jagow; Falkenhayn, also, the Chief of the Great General Staff, and next to him,

Von Tirpitz, creator and controlling mind of the German Navy. Present also was the chief of the German Secret Service, and last, but not least, the Chief of the German Official Press Bureau.

Von Buelow had scarcely taken his seat when the murmur of desultory conversation suddenly ceased, and every man stiffened to the habitual pose of military and state decorum, as the Kaiser entered and strode to the head of the table.

Was he changed by the tragic happenings of the last twenty months? Yes, and no. The hair had whitened, and the stupendous burden of responsibility had bowed somewhat, as well it might, the shoulders upon which it had borne so heavily. But there was something in that flashing blue eye, in the set of the lips, and in the whole atmosphere of that ever-to-be-remembered face, which showed that he was still a Prussian of the Prussians, and

that the indomitable spirit of the latest,
if not the last of the Hohenzollerns,
burned unquenched and unquenchable in
the soul of the man.

Obeying the scarcely perceptible wave
of his hand, the distinguished company
seated themselves with their Kaiser for a
council which, as subsequent events
proved with lightning-like rapidity, was
to be big with the fate, not this time of
Europe, but of the great Western Hemisphere.

And thus he spoke:

" The Day has come and gone and Germany has lost! What may have been and
what yet may be the purposes of an in-
scrutable Providence neither you nor I can
tell. This much I do know, that if the
sword was thrust into our hands by the
Almighty for our own chastisement, it is
for us to bow our heads in submission.
That God sent us into battle for our own

permanent undoing, I do not believe. Our
beloved Fatherland has set up before the
eyes of the world a *kultur* too broad and
beneficent, and the influence of that *kultur*
upon the great world outside of Germany
has been too profound and will prove too
lasting, for God ever to contemplate the
fall and passing away of the great German Empire. As surely as gold is purified
by fire, so surely shall Germany emerge,
freed of all dross and with more splendid
potentialities for the future, out of this
seven-times heated furnace of the war.

" I ask you to consider that Germany has
passed through this supreme ordeal with
her vitality unimpaired and her military
prestige enhanced. I will even say that
she is the stronger for her territorial
losses. Alsace and Lorraine have ever
been a thorn in the side of Germany—
the one impassable barrier to cordial relations with our great French neighbor,

whose good will, as you well know, it has
been my earnest endeavor to win. And
as for our lost colonial possessions, I, as
well as you, have long recognized that they
were too widely scattered, too little co-
ordinated, to carry much military value;
moreover, as outlets for our expanding
population, they have failed of their purpose.

"Of the crime of Kiao-Chou I will say
no more than that Germany never forgets!

"Has Germany, then, no future beyond
the seas? She has, most assuredly, and it
lies (would that we had recognized the
fact, and recognizing, acted upon it long
ago) in the Western Hemisphere, in the
southern half of the great American con-
tinent. South America beckons the German colonist and calls to us for the further
exploitation of its abundant natural resources by that combination of German
science, capital, and organization, with

which our competitors have found it impossible sucessfully to compete.

" But if, by purchase or by such means as the time and circumstance may demand, we are to found a colony or colonies in South America, it will be necessary to clear the air by disposing, once and for all, of that curious fiction which has come to be known as the ' Monroe Doctrine.' The peculiar claims set forth therein by the United States have been described as ' the most magnificent bluff in all history and, so far, the most successful.' But you and I know, and it is known in all the chancellories of Europe, that the bravado has been successful only by our sufferance, and because the great problems of Europe, for which the late war has been fought, called for more pressing solution.

" I have spoken of the ' Monroe Doctrine ' as a fiction—perhaps I had better have described it as composed of many fic-

tions, not the least among which has been
the belief that back of this policy lay the
strength of the British fleet. I know not
with certainty how much of truth there has
been in that assumption; but, thanks to the
work of our plenipotentiary at Geneva, an
understanding, secret and supplementary
to the general treaty, was reached with the
British representative, by which, in consideration of our withdrawal from the
Euphrates Valley (which the collapse of
the Turkish Empire has rendered less at-
tractive to German enterprise than it
was), Great Britain pledges herself to a
neutral attitude on the ' Monroe Doctrine,'
except so far as it affects her own North
American possessions.

"With the fleet of Great Britain elimi-
nated as an element in the problem, it be-
comes possible for Germany, as I shall
show you later, to achieve, through the
instrumentality of her fleet, a feat of arms

which, in a swift series of operations, shall restore our naval and military prestige in the eyes of the German people, demolish for all time the ' Monroe Doctrine,' and transfer from the shoulders of Germany to those of the United States of America the burden of the fifteen-billion-dollar indemnity, imposed upon us by the Treaty to which, only yesterday, we appended our signature.

" I have said that the war has added to our military prestige—I will go further and say that, in the eyes of all the world, and particularly among those who follow the profession of arms, our military prestige has been immeasurably increased. We set out to fight the two greatest military powers, next to ourselves; and alone we would have crushed them utterly. As the event has proved, Germany and Austria found themselves confronted by the embattled hosts of no less than ten nations.

Nevertheless, we carried the war into the enemy's territory, and, so far as Germany is concerned, we presented an impregnable wall, which was finally pierced, only by overwhelming numbers, and, thanks largely to our American friends, by a preponderance of artillery against which even the indomitable soldiers of Germany could not prevail.

" It is only by the mass of the German people that these things are not well understood. We, of the ruling class, you will remember, told the people, brought up as they were to believe in the absolute invincibility of the German army, that within a month of the declaration of war we should be in Paris and within two months in St. Petersburg. Instead, they have seen that army arrested, held fast, and finally thrown back in defeat upon its own borders. The Socialists of Germany, working upon the minds of a defeated and discouraged people, are laying the blame for this disaster upon the shoulders of the very class which has made Germany what it is. We, it is, who have made the German Empire and given to it the only system of government which, bearing in mind the century-long training and peculiar temperament of its people, can maintain it intact amid the powerful and jealous nations of Europe, and carry it forward to the greater future that awaits it.

"The prestige of the army and navy and the confidence of the people in its ruling class can be restored only by some swift and brilliant feat of arms—and in view of the rapidly augmenting strength of the Socialistic upheaval, that feat of arms cannot be performed too soon.

"The United States, as you are well aware, has recently reaffirmed the 'Monroe Doctrine' by definite Congressional action, forbidding the acquisition by any

alien power of harbors or coaling stations
which are located within striking distance
of the Panama Canal, and which might
serve as a base for hostile operations in
the Caribbean.

"That, gentlemen, is a clear and bold—
I had almost said defiant—expression of
one of the most important among the
great foreign policies which the United
States, since the period of the Spanish
War, has adopted and proclaimed to the
world in no unmeasured terms. In addition to the 'Monroe Doctrine' I have but
to refer to their championship of the
'Open Door' in China, to the matter of
the exclusion of the Asiatics, and to the
construction and fortification of the Panama Canal; which great work and the
Caribbean, as I foresee it, in the future
naval wars of the New World, will be
what Gibraltar and the Mediterranean
were to the contending navies of the eight-

eenth century.   The ultimate entry of the
great republic of the Western Hemisphere
into the field of world politics was, of
course, inevitable; but that this entrance
would be marked by the adoption of a line
of policies so bold as these, involving the
possibility, nay the certainty, of conflict
sooner or later with the great naval and
military powers of the world, I, for one,
was not prepared to believe.

"Had there been in the United States
that intimate and well-balanced relation-
ship and co-operation between the diplomatic and the naval and military services
which obtains in Germany, the growth of
these ambitious policies would have been
marked by a commensurate growth of the
military and naval forces of the country.
This co-operation, as you are well aware,
has been conspicuously absent.   The
United States Congress, always fearful
and jealous of what it is pleased to term

'militarism,' has failed to listen to the warnings of its military advisers; with the result, to-day, that it is endeavoring to support a line of first-class international policies with a third-class navy, and with military forces which are so insignificant that, in the eyes of a first-class military nation, they may be regarded as practically negligible. The burden of responsibility for these conditions lies not upon the naval and military advisers of Congress, but upon Congress itself; which, as our ambassadors have from time to time informed us, does not hesitate to play politics with matters which involve the very life and death of the nation itself.

" Should the blow which Germany, in the hour of her dire need, is about to strike against the United States lead that great country to a realization of the necessity at all times for proper naval and military preparedness, the regret which I and Germany feel at having to break our friendly relations with a country with which we have always lived in perfect amity, will be tempered by the thought that, out of her temporary loss she will reap a future gain of inestimable benefit.

" It is noteworthy that our swift descent upon that great country could not be carried out with any reasonable hope of success, had the United States Congress but given heed to the words of its first soldier-president which were spoken, if my memory serves me well, in his first annual address. ' To be prepared for war,' said Washington, ' is one of the most effectual means of preserving peace. A free people ought not only to be armed, but disciplined; to which end a uniform and well-digested plan is requisite.' "

The Kaiser ceased speaking and, turning to the Foreign Secretary, he said: " Von Jagow, have you had the necessary conversations with the Danish minister, and have you requested him to be present?"

"The conversations were eminently satisfactory, your Majesty. The Danish minister is in the anteroom and awaits your commands."

"Send for him," said the Kaiser.

The Danish minister entered, and he was no sooner seated than the Kaiser, without any preliminaries, abruptly asked, "What sum do you name as the purchase price of the island of St. Thomas in the West Indies?"

"Twenty-five million dollars, your Majesty," said the minister.

"We will give you that sum for the island," said the Kaiser. "The only stipulation is that you shall pledge yourself to secrecy, leaving it to Germany to announce, at such time as may seem best, the transfer of the island. Here are the necessary

papers, and if you will affix your signature
the transfer can be consummated here and
now."

The Danish minister smiled, took the
pen, signed the documents, and, after the
customary felicitations, withdrew.

III

AN UNDEFENDED TREASURE LAND

"GENTLEMEN," said the Kaiser, as the door closed upon the retiring Danish minister, "I have frequently said to you in this council chamber that the future of Germany lies upon the sea. To-day, in spite of the enforced inaction of our fleet during the war, I hold to that doctrine with unshaken conviction. Hence I did not hesitate, Von Buelow, to instruct you to offer fifteen billion dollars as the price of redeeming the fleet.

"If you ask me, as all Germany, doubtless, is asking itself at this very hour, how it will be possible for our stricken Fatherland to discharge this enormous obligation, I answer that not a single pfennig of this indemnity shall be raised by the taxation

of my beloved people, or be paid out of
their national treasury.

" Gentlemen, you may rest assured that
when I authorized the acceptance of the
indemnity, I had already determined on
a plan by which this stupendous sum could
be realized without adding to the heavy
obligations which the war had already imposed upon us."

Springing to his feet, the Kaiser swept
his outstretched arm to the westward, and
his voice took on that incisive staccato
which indicates in him the deepest feeling:
"On yonder side of the Atlantic lies an
undefended treasure land, fifty billions of
whose one hundred and fifty billions of
wealth are to be found on the seaboard,
and within easy reach of an expeditionary
force and the guns of a hostile fleet. It is
my purpose that the German Navy, on
whose behalf I have assumed the indemnity, shall be made the instrument for se-

curing the means of payment. It will ap-
peal to your sense of the fitness of things
that the United States, which has con-
tributed so largely to our defeat, should
pay the costs of this war and that the navy
should play the part of collector.

" If it should be said that this descent
upon the coasts of the United States is a
premeditated attack upon a friendly power,
our reply will be, that, though the charge
is technically true, ethically it is false.
When that neutral country turned itself
into an arsenal for the supply of guns,
ammunition, and military stores and equipment to the enemies of Germany, it became in effect an active participant in our
overthrow. You, Von Falkenhayn, will
agree with me that the military supplies
furnished to the Allies by the United
States were of more value to them than
several army corps. It was the preponderance of artillery, due in large measure to

the purchases from America, that was the
ultimate cause of our loss of the war.

"Although it was technically correct and
in agreement with international law, the
material assistance rendered by the United
States was, I repeat, morally wrong; and
in sending my fleet to exact from that
country both the indemnity and the cost to
Germany of the war, or twenty billion dollars in all, I feel that I am performing no
more than an act of righteous retribution.

" The object of our expedition will be
greatly facilitated by the fact that the
dreadnought fleet of the United States,
consisting of ten ships, is now assembled
off Vera Cruz—the Washington Government being still engaged in toying with the
Mexican situation by following out its
futile policy of 'Watchful waiting.'
Equally favorable to our plans is the fact
that the bulk of the effective regular force
of 30,000 men in the Continental United

States is gathered on the Mexican border.
The pre-dreadnought fleet of the United
States, moreover, is being paraded, just
now, in the various ports of the Pacific
Coast.

" You, Von Tirpitz, will agree with me
that the prolonged inactivity of our fleet
in the North Sea and Baltic ports has rendered it desirable that the ships be at once
sent to sea for a series of maneuvers on a
grand scale, the operations to extend over
a series of weeks.

" After a grand review, which I shall
hold off Heligoland, the fleet will be dispatched to the Atlantic, ostensibly for
these maneuvers, but actually for a descent
upon the coasts of the United States.

" From a rendezvous in the western Atlantic, the various divisions of the main
fleet will move to the selected points of
attack in accordance with the general plans
formulated several years ago as the result

of our academic study of the problem of an invasion of the United States. The modifications necessary for the present enterprise will be such as are rendered necessary by the present strength of our fleet, the location and strength of the enemy's forces, and by the imperative demand for secrecy, dispatch, and strict coordination as to time and place.

That, gentlemen, is the plan and April 1, 1916, will be '*Der Tag!*'"

IV

EMBARKATION OF THE GERMAN ARMY

UPON the declaration of peace, the German Government announced that the military rule and censorship which had obtained throughout the war would be extended to cover the few weeks which would be required for the demobilization of the German army. It was explained that this course was adopted for the double purpose of facilitating the orderly return of the citizen-soldiers to their homes, and of delaying any publication of the strength of the German army in the field at the close of the war, and of its total losses, until such time as the government thought best to make these facts public.

On the very day, March 1st, of the sign-

ing of the Peace of Geneva, and in some
cases even while the ink of the signatories
was wet upon the paper, the great fleet of
German merchant ships which had been interned in foreign ports during the war
cast loose its moorings and set sail for the
Fatherland.   Among the first of these
ships to start out from her pier and head
for the open sea was the great Hamburg-
American liner *Vaterland*, and as she
and the *Kaiser Wilhelm II*, of the North
German Lloyd, followed at intervals
by other ships of these two companies,
steamed down the North River, and out
through the Narrows, New York wished
them Godspeed on their homeward voyage
with the flying of flags, the dipping of en-
signs by the shipping, and the prolonged
roar of a thousand steam whistles and
sirens.

Meanwhile in Germany all public traffic
over the railways was suspended and the

huge task of returning some seven millions
of men to their homes was begun.

Not all of the troops, however, were
thus immediately redistributed to the
farms and factories and business houses of
Germany. A picked force of 200,000
veterans of the first line was diverted to
the leading German seaports on the North
Sea and the Baltic, and within a few days
after the close of the war 20,000 of these
troops, with the necessary artillery and
equipment, had been embarked upon certain transports of moderate size and draft,
which, as soon as the troops were aboard,
pulled out into midstream and awaited
further orders. In every case the troops
went aboard at night, and during the operation the cordon of secrecy drawn around
the various naval bases and ports at which
the embarkation took place was tightened.

While the loaded transports were awaiting their orders, the troops remained be-

low deck and only the regular working force of the ship was visible. One by one, and from widely separated harbors, these ships slipped their moorings and put to sea. Some by the way of the English Channel and others following the route around the north coast of Scotland and Ireland, they proceeded at slow speed to their appointed rendezvous in the western Atlantic.

Each ship sailed at sundown, and during the first night out the color and banding of its smokestacks were changed to that of some foreign ship of similar size and contour, the corresponding foreign flag being flown. Those that took the southerly route regulated their speed so as to pass through the straits of Dover at night; those that laid their course around the north of Scotland maintained a good offing, beyond signaling distance of the coast guard and signal stations. As soon as it was well clear of the Channel and the Irish coast, each ship, avoiding the regular sailing routes, laid its course to the westward.

Meanwhile the work of transforming the largest and fastest of the German ocean liners, headed by the *Imperator* and her recently-completed sister ship, the new *Bismarck,* into transports was being rushed day and night by the largest working force that could be crowded upon their decks. The commodious, first-class staterooms were stripped of their furniture and galvanized-pipe folding berths were fitted on each wall. The spacious saloons, restaurants, palm gardens, etc., were similarly denuded of their furnishings and fitted with berths. The wide promenade decks were inclosed by canvas and fitted with berthing accommodation. So vast is the space available on the nine decks and in the holds of these ships, which in peace

time can carry 5,000 souls, that when
the alterations were completed, it was
found that each of the three ships of the
Imperator class could carry 10,000 troops
with their full equipment.

The work of transforming the liners
that had been interned in the United
States began on the day they left New
York, and they were stripped and ready
for the shipyard workmen by the time,
seven days later, they reached the home
ports. With such efficiency and dispatch
was this work carried through that the
second expeditionary force of 50,000 men
was embarked and had sailed on or before
the 28th of March. The transports
carrying this force were vessels of from
20 to 23 knots' speed. Some of them sailed
boldly on advertised schedules, direct for
New York; the rest slipped away by night,
adopting the same ruses and secrecy as the
transports of the first expedition. They

sailed at intervals during the last two
weeks of March, and the rate of steaming
was so adjusted as to bring the whole expedition to New York, Boston, and Washington between the 1st and 3d of April.

The third army of 130,000 men, in
transports of from 14 to 19 knots' speed
set sail on April 1st, the faster ships of
the *George Washington* and *America* type
pushing on with all speed, and the slower
ships proceeding as a fleet under convoy
of the ten battleships of the *Wittlesbach*
and *Kaiser Wilhelm II.* classes.

And so it came about that, by employ-
ing the full force of every naval and private shipyard in the country, Germany,
within the month, had embarked upon the
seas an army of invasion composed of
200,000 of the picked veteran troops of
the war, completely equipped with artillery, transport, and supplies.

And, thanks to the tightening of the

censorship and the patriotic silence of the shipyard employees, not a whisper of what was going on escaped to the outside world, until on April 1st the third expeditionary force, convoyed by battleships, steamed boldly out into the North Sea and laid its course by way of the English Channel for the coasts of America.

V

THE GERMAN FLEET SETS SAIL

On March 15th, there was published in the leading Berlin papers, and repeated throughout the world, the following official announcement: "The restoration of peace, the return of our valiant army, and the fact that our navy has emerged from the war with its strength unimpaired, will be celebrated by a grand review of the whole German fleet which will be held in the Bight of Heligoland, in the presence of the Kaiser. At the conclusion of the review, in order to afford the fleet an opportunity, on an extended scale, for those exercises on the high seas which have been denied to it because of the overwhelming strength of the enemy, it will set sail for a series of grand maneuvers.

" The operations will be based upon the
theory that a powerful enemy's fleet is approaching the coast of Europe from the
westward for the purpose of finding, and,
if possible, destroying the German fleet.
Early information of this movement having reached the Admiralty, our fleet has
been dispatched to seek out and, if possible, destroy the enemy (which has been
reported as somewhere in the mid-At-
lantic), before he shall have reached European waters. Our forces will be about
equally divided into the attacking, or Red
fleet, and the defending, or Blue fleet. Immediately after the review, the Red fleet
will steam to the westward, and when it
has reached a designated position, will
commence its approach. Thirty-six hours
later the defending, or Blue fleet will be
dispatched to meet the enemy."

The morning of March 18th revealed,
drawn up under the lee of Heligoland, the

greatest naval force that had ever assembled under the German flag. Anchored in five long parallel lines, it covered many square miles of the calm waters of the Bight; and the ships, glistening in a new coat of paint, showed up, under the brilliant sun of that bright spring morning, with all the picturesqueness and air of gaiety befitting a great national pageant.

The first line, six miles in length, was made up of dreadnoughts and battle-cruisers, the second line of pre-dread-nought battleships, the third of armored cruisers and light cruisers, the fourth of destroyers and seagoing submarines, and the fifth of the auxiliaries.

Promptly at the hour of twelve, the Kaiser, from the bridge of the *Hohen-zollern,* opened the review, and as he made his way up and down those far-flung lines, ship after ship thundered forth its volleys in honor of the man to whom, despite the recent reverses of Germany, the hearts of his people turned with faith unshaken.

After the *Hohenzollern* had made the circuit of the fleet, she steamed a couple of miles to the westward, and anchored. Then the ships of the Red fleet, composed of the eight dreadnoughts of the *Thuringen* and *Nassau* classes, the battle-cruisers, twelve light cruisers, and thirty seagoing destroyers, weighed anchor and saluted the Kaiser, as they steamed into the North Sea on their way to the English Channel.

When the flagship had passed the *Hohenzollern,* the admiral in command of the fleet opened his sealed orders, which read as follows: " As soon as it is clear of the English Channel, the Red fleet, avoiding the customary steamship routes, will proceed at slow speed to the Caribbean, reaching a position 50 miles to the south of the island of Hayti by April 5th. Here

the Red fleet will await further orders,
which will reach it in due course by wireless from the Commander-in-Chief of the
Blue fleet."

Thirty-six hours after the sailing of
the Red fleet the Blue fleet set sail. It
consisted of the nine dreadnoughts of
the *Koenig* and *Kaiser* classes, the armored cruisers, twelve light cruisers of 23
to 27 knots' speed, forty destroyers, and
the whole of the thirty seagoing submarines. The sealed orders of the admiral read as follows: "After clearing the
English Channel, the Blue fleet will proceed on a course midway between the fre-
quented lines of steamship travel, until it
reaches the thirty-fifth parallel. It will
then proceed due west until it reaches a
point of rendezvous 250 miles from the
coast of the United States. Here it will
meet a fleet of transports carrying 20,000
troops. At the point of rendezvous the

six groups of submarines will replenish
their fuel tanks, and proceed to the respec-
tive points of attack assigned to them at
such speeds as to bring them off the various
harbors at sundown on the night of March
31st. During the night they will enter,
assume favorable positions for attack,
and, where conditions allow, will go to
sleep on the bottom until the dawn of
April 1st.

"The transports will proceed in scattered
formation from the rendezvous to the
various points of landing, steaming at such
a speed that they will be off the coast and
within two hours' steaming of the landing
places at sundown on March 31st.

The battleship divisions will reach the
entrance to the harbors of the cities which
they are to lay under tribute at dawn on
April 1st. They will remain outside the
extreme range of the coast fortifications'
guns, and at a signal that our landing

forces have possession of the forts, they
will enter and take position for bombardment of the cities."

And so, on March 20, 1916, in the
dark of a moonless night, the last ship of
the greatest naval raid ever planned in the
history of the world headed silently from
the Bight of Heligoland for the North
Sea and the coast of North America!

VI

ON the morning of March 20th, there appeared in the morning papers of the United States a dispatch from Berlin, stating that negotiations were believed to be under way between the governments of Germany and Denmark, having in view the purchase by Germany of the Danish island of St. Thomas in the West Indies. " This movement," read the dispatch, " is the first step in a policy of the German Empire of acquiring, by purchase, certain coaling and refitting stations for the use of its great merchant marine, whose activities, released by the Peace of Geneva, are once more in full swing. Germany realizes and accepts the new conditions which have been brought about by the great war. For the future,

the resources, energy, and skill of the German people will be directed less to naval
and military achievements and more than
ever to the upbuilding and enlargement of
her internal industries, the multiplication
of the ships of her merchant marine, and
the greater extension of her trade and
commerce in all the countries of the
world."

On the following morning there appeared in one of the leading New York
dailies the following letter from Washington: "Had not yesterday's dispatch from
Berlin, stating that negotiations were under
way for the purchase by Germany of the
Danish West Indian Island of St. Thomas,
been given such unusually widespread pub-
licity, the matter would not have attracted
the serious attention which is being devoted
to it in Washington. It is the general im-
pression in well-informed circles in this city
that the tone of the dispatch and its world-

wide circulation bear the earmarks of the German official press bureau. Were it not for this, its moderate and pacific tone would carry more conviction. Be that as it may, the least that can be done is to take the assurances of Germany's new point of view as to her destiny at their face value. The serious side of this matter for the Government of the United States, however, is not the question as to what will be Germany's future world policy, so much as the fact that the suggested purchase of St. Thomas, should it take place, would be a broad violation of the principles of the ' Monroe Doctrine,' and a very direct challenge to the reaffirmation by Congress of that Doctrine, with particular respect to the waters and territory adjacent to the Panama Canal and therefore within easy striking distance of the same. It is stated in well-informed quarters that our foreign office has lost no time in directing its Ambassa-

dor in Berlin to make the necessary official
inquiry and, if necessary, follow it up with
the strongest representations to the German Government."

On March 24th the representatives of
the leading papers throughout the country
were invited to meet the Secretary of State,
who wished to make a communication on the
subject of St. Thomas. They found him
in the very best of humor, and he stated
that he was pleased to tell them, that the
slight cloud which had settled down upon
the mutual relations of the United States
and Germany had been completely dis-
pelled by the announcement of the German Government, that no negotiations of
any kind whatsoever were in progress for
the purchase of the Danish West India
Island of St. Thomas.

One week later the early editions of the
evening papers of March 31st displayed in
full-face headlines the news, that the Ger-

man Government had announced that it had purchased St. Thomas and that it proposed to make of it one of the strongest naval bases in the world.

At the call of the President, a meeting of the Cabinet convened that night at the White House at 9 P.M. In view of the crisis, the members of the Cabinet arrived early, eager to ascertain from the Secretary of State the facts of the grave diplomatic situation. From him they learned, informally, that, having returned late that afternoon from lecturing in the West on " The Perils of Militarism," he was able to find time only for brief interviews with the German and the British Ambassadors. The German Ambassador had informed him that the dispatch published in the afternoon papers was essentially correct.

The President entered, seated himself, and at once asked the Secretary of State to give the latest information available from his department. " I have to inform you, sir, that the German Ambassador practically confirms the Berlin dispatch, and that, in my opinion, the island of St. Thomas is at this hour the property of the German Government."

" In that case, gentlemen," said the President, " the situation is free from any ambiguity. By the purchase of St. Thomas, in the face of our recent protest, Germany challenges one of the most vital policies of the United States. The issues are clean-cut; either Germany must abrogate this sale, or we must abandon the ' Monroe Doctrine,' or the matter must be submitted to the test of war."

" I am for peace," said the Secretary of the Navy; " but I believe that our answer to this affront should be a sharp ultimatum offering to Germany the alternative of a return of St. Thomas to Denmark or— war! Germany will never dare to fight us over the 'Monroe Doctrine'; for she knows that back of that policy lies not only our own battle-fleet but that of Great Britain as well."

"Can the Secretary of State give us any definite assurance as to Great Britain's attitude?" asked the President.

"I had a conversation with the British Ambassador before coming to this meeting, relative to the attitude of Great Britain in the event of hostilities. He stated that he was advised by his government that the failure of the United States Government to make any protest against the violation of Belgian neutrality, or against the strewing of mines on the high seas, the bombardment of peaceful villages and undefended coast towns, and other violations of the humanitarian laws of war, had so far estranged the sympathies of the British nation that the most its government could pledge itself to, in the event of our becoming embroiled with

Germany over the 'Monroe Doctrine,' was an attitude of strict neutrality."

Of all the men around that board the President alone seemed to realize the tremendous significance of this announcement. He bowed his head in deep thought, oblivious, for the time, to the discussion among the members as to whether Germany, exhausted as she must be by the terrific struggle of the past twenty months, would be willing and able to take up arms almost before she had laid them down.

Suddenly, and with powerful emphasis, the President said:

" Gentlemen, would it not be more sane and more consistent with the dignity of the Cabinet if, instead of indulging in speculation as to whether Germany would fight, we find out definitely whether we are in a position to do so ourselves." Turning to the Secretary of War and the Secretary of the Navy, he said: " Send for the Chief of

Staff of the Army and the President of the
General Board of the Navy, and I will ask
for their expert opinion as to our preparedness for a conflict with the greatest military and second greatest naval power in
the world."

Immediately upon their entrance the
President said: " I have asked your attendance here, so that I may inform you that
the Secretary of State has learned that the
purchase of St. Thomas by Germany has
been accomplished, and that the British
Government has made it clear that, in the
event of war over this violation of the
' Monroe Doctrine,' it can pledge itself
only to an attitude of strict neutrality. The
questions have arisen, first, as to whether
Germany, in view of her defeat in the recent struggle, would be willing to risk another war; and, second, as to whether, if
she did, our naval and military forces are
in such a condition of strength and pre-

paredness as to warrant our entertaining a reasonable hope of carrying it to a successful issue."

The first to reply was the President of the General Board of the Navy: " In a crisis so serious as this I presume, Mr. President, that you wish me to speak with absolute candor and without reserve. There is no reason to suppose that Germany has emerged from this war exhausted and broken down. Her main fleet having remained within her ports throughout the war, is not only intact, but has been increased by the addition of several dreadnoughts of the most modern design. Some light cruisers also have been added, together with a considerable number of sea-going destroyers and submarines of the largest and latest type. So far as her main fleet is concerned, there can be no doubt that it is stronger and even better prepared for battle than it was at the commencement of the late war. With the menace of the British fleet removed, Germany is free to concentrate on our coast the whole strength of her navy. The General Board has reason to believe that Germany several years ago worked out a plan for the invasion of the United States, and it is believed also that, in the event of war, she would strike at once with all her available forces. It would be her object to overwhelm our fleet, obtain command of the sea, and land an expeditionary force, say, of 150,000 to 200,000 men, which, if our fleet were destroyed, she would be able to accomplish within ten or twelve days from the commencement of hostilities. The decisive action would have to be fought between the dreadnought fleets of the two nations, and, if we gave battle, we should find ourselves opposed by a fighting line of double the strength of our own; for Germany can oppose twenty dreadnoughts to our ten, and judging from such

naval actions as were fought in the late
war, in which both the gunnery and the
seamanship of the Germans were excellent,
there can be little doubt that with such
great odds against us, we should be defeated.   Had the Congress in past years
seen fit to listen to the warnings of the
Board, and built up a fleet sufficient for the
defence of the United States, we should
have been prepared at this hour to match
ship with ship and gun with gun.

" The seriousness of the situation is ag-
gravated by the fact that all of the ships of
our pre-dreadnought classes in commission
are now distributed in the various ports of
the Pacific Coast, and therefore will not be
available to meet that swift attack which
the enemy would undoubtedly make immediately upon the declaration of war.   This
division of the fleet was opposed to the very
first principles of naval strategy, and it
was done against the strongest protest of

this Board, backed by the judgment of every naval officer of the service. Mr. President, I have answered your question, and I repeat, first, that the German Navy is in a state of the highest preparedness and efficiency; secondly, that despite the excellence of our ships and the high quality of our officers and men, the relative weakness of our navy and the wide dispersion of its forces, to say nothing of the shortage of men and officers and lack of adequate reserves, would render a successful issue to the war practically impossible."

The President of the General Board took his seat amid a profound silence.

He was followed by the Chief of Staff of the Army, who said: " In answer to your first question, Mr. President, as to whether Germany, having emerged from a great war, would be ready to undertake another, I have this to say: that all history teaches us that a nation never fights more

readily and valiantly than immediately
after the close of a war in which it was
involved. In proof of this I would call
your attention to the fact that the North
showed no signs of being exhausted by the
Civil War in the sense of being unready
for further military effort. On the contrary, it was the possession of a great army
of well-trained and veteran soldiers, amply
equipped and provided with all the muni-
tions of war, that enabled her to assume an
uncompromising attitude to France over the
Mexican difficulty. So far from exhausting
Russia, the unsuccessful war which that
country waged against Japan redounded
greatly to her benefit; so much so, that
when the recent war opened, the morale of
her army was higher than ever before, and
in equipment, arms, and organization she
proved to be one of the great surprises of
that conflict. Even the little kingdom of
Servia fought first Turkey, then Bulgaria,

and finally, and with scarcely a spell of rest, she waged the most remarkable campaign of her history against a first-class military power.

" In the event of the probable defeat of our fleet due to scattered forces and the overwhelming strength of the enemy, Germany would at once commence the invasion of our territory. And the question which I have been called here to answer is: what would be our chances of successfully resisting such an invasion and driving the enemy back to the sea?

" We have at the present hour, within the Continental United States, only about 30,000 men of the regular army, including mobile troops, cavalry, infantry, and field artillery; and we have about 16,000 men manning the coast defences, which is about one-half the necessary number. In the militia of the United States, which totals 127,000 men and officers on paper, only

104,000 are actually mustered. Of these
104,000, only some 60,000 are ready for
immediate service in the field; so that our
total forces in the United States consist of
16,000 men scattered in the coast defences
throughout our Atlantic, Gulf, and Pacific
Coast fortifications, which would not be
available for service in the field; 30,000
regulars and 60,000 militia. That is to
say, our mobile troops capable of taking
the field number only 90,000 men, and
these, we must remember, are scattered
from Maine to California and from Canada
to the Gulf.

" In the event of invasion by Germany in
great force, with a thoroughly equipped
army provided with the full complement of
field-guns, howitzers, and other necessary
equipment, the first contingent of which
expeditionary force might readily amount to
150,000 veterans of the late war, where
should we stand? It would be an optimistic

forecast for me to say that we could concentrate these 90,000 men at any point on the Atlantic Coast within thirty days of the declaration of war. And when the concentration had been made, the troops would be without properly trained artillery and cavalry organization, and without ammunition trains; they would be hastily organized and assembled for the first time in large bodies; they would be unprepared to act effectively as an army; and should these troops be defeated, the country would have back of them practically no reserve of men and supplies. There is a shortage of men and guns in the regular field artillery; we possess less than half the needed militia field batteries; and it would require three months of training to render what we have efficient.

" Practically all of our coast fortifications can be taken in reverse. Many of them to-day are manned only by a few com-

panies, and it would be possible for the
enemy, by a night landing and surprise attack, to capture the fortifications from the
rear, thus rendering it possible for the enemy's fleet to enter our harbors and lay
our seacoast cities under tribute. With our
seacoast cities and fortifications in the
hands of the enemy, it would be possible
for him, having at hand unlimited transport, a vast army, and complete equipment,
to land in the first week of the war sufficient forces to capture all the arsenals, ammunition, supplies, and factories for the
manufacture of guns, rifles, and powder,
long before our widely-scattered mobile
army of 30,000 regulars and 60,000 militia
could be brought together, effectively to
stay his progress. Modern wars, Mr.
President, are machine-made, and without
the proper machinery war cannot be waged.
You, Mr. Secretary of State, have recently
affirmed that such is the patriotism of our

people, that you could raise an army of one million men between sun and sun; but I tell you that your million men, without the proper equipment of artillery and the other machinery of war, would be but a mob one million strong. Before I take my seat, Mr. President, I shall make so bold as to suggest to you in this hour of great peril (in which I see you actually facing the very crisis and conditions against which my predecessors in office have warned the country and its Congress for many years past), that the naval, and particularly the military situation, is such that, in his dealings with the German Government, it would be advisable that your Secretary of State should put on kid gloves of the very softest texture."

And the Secretary of State did so.

But, six hours after that Cabinet meeting closed, Germany declared war on the United States.

VII

REPORT from the Commander of the German Submarine U-40 to the Commander-in-Chief of the Imperial German Expeditionary Fleet at New York:

> Flagship U-40,
> New York,
> April 1, 1916.

Commander-in-Chief, Imperial German Expeditionary Fleet, New York.

Sir:—I have the honor to report that, following your instructions, my flotilla, consisting of U-40, U-41, and U-42, made the entrance to the Ambrose Channel, Port of New York, on the evening of March 31, shortly after 11 P.M. No moon, sky overcast. Proceeded at surface at half speed, in line ahead; interval three hundred yards; leading boats showing hooded lights astern to preserve station.

At entrance to the Narrows flotilla submerged and proceeded at one-third speed, reaching New York Navy Yard at 4:30 A.M., April 1st.

I submit a rough sketch showing the position of the drydocks and of the enemy's vessels, and also the course followed by the boats of my flotilla.

In a conference held aboard our tender before reaching the American coast, I arranged that U-40 should attack the submarines and destroyers; that U-41 should torpedo the caisson gate of drydock A; and that U-42 should destroy the gate of drydock B. Each boat was to do such other damage as the conditions would permit. U-40 and U-41 were to enter in line ahead, and make the circuit of the basin; U-42 was to back in and take position in the middle of the basin.

Flagship U-40 led the way in at 4:45
A.M. Sighted dreadnought at C, a battleship in drydock A, three submarines
abreast at D, three destroyers at E, two
destroyers alongside pier at F, and a
battleship at G. On approaching the end
of basin, U-40 turned hard to port, stopping port motor, and as the enemy submarines and destroyers came on the bearing (See No. 1 on plan) discharged my
two bow torpedoes. Secured effective
hits. As I swung around, brought stern
tubes to bear on two destroyers at Pier F
(No. 2) and scored hits with two torpedoes. Then brought battleship on the
bearing (No. 3), and struck her on port
bow.

U-41, following 200 yards astern,
swung around in my wake, and, upon
bringing gate of Dock A on the bearing,
discharged stern tubes and made a fair
hit (No. 4). To avoid being swept into

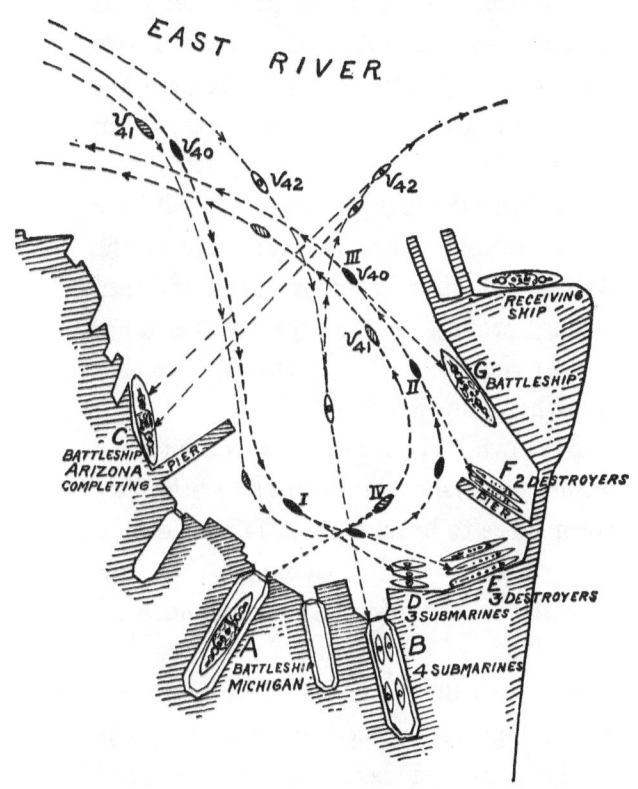

SKETCH SHOWING COURSE OF SUBMARINES IN THE
ATTACK ON BROOKLYN NAVY YARD.

the dock by rush of water, port motor was started; and, although U-41 was drawn back almost to the entrance, she held her own, and turning to port followed me out of the basin.

Looking through periscope, I could see the battleship (since ascertained to be the *Michigan*), first lifted by the stern, then swung around and swept to the inner end of the dock. In my opinion, the ship must be badly wrecked.

Meanwhile U-42 had backed into the basin, and maneuvering so as to bring her stern tubes to bear, made a fair hit on the gate of Drydock B. Coming to the surface for better vision, her commander reports that, over the crest of the wave that rushed into the dock, he was able to see four submarines picked up from the floor of the dock and dashed against its inner end. As U-42 was leaving the basin, she turned to starboard, bringing her stern tubes to bear on a big dreadnought, since ascertained to be the *Pennsylvania*, that was completing construction alongside wharf at C, and struck her with two torpedoes, one amidships and another on the bow. As we passed down the East River, we could see by the inclination of her masts that she was heeling rapidly to starboard. She is probably now on the bottom.

Our work being thus completed, we came to the surface, proceeded to the upper bay and joined the destroyer flotilla, as directed.

I wish to commend to your favorable attention the excellent work of my own crew and of the commanders and crews of U-41 and U-42, who carried out their instructions with great dash and precision and with complete success.

I have the honor to be
    Yours obediently,
R. Schlesinger, Lieutenant, I. G. N.

Report from Commander W. Neumann
of the Submarine U-30 to the Commander-
in-Chief of the German Fleet at New
York:

Flagship U-30,
Limon Bay,
Panama Canal Zone,
April 1, 1916.
Commander-in-Chief, Imperial German
Expeditionary Fleet, New York.

Sir:—I have the honor to report, that
following your instructions, my flotilla,
consisting of U-30, U-31, U-32, reached
Limon Bay, Panama Canal Zone, at night-
fall, March 31st, convoyed by the light
cruiser *Rostock*. At 3 A.M., April 1st, proceeded at the surface, under electric
motors, through the dredged entrance to
the canal, laying our course by the canal
range lights, which we found to be ex-
cellently placed. When off Cristobal,

dropped U-32 for its attack on enemy submarine flotilla and proceeded cautiously. It had previously been arranged that U-30 should attack the easterly and U-31 the westerly gates. Sighted Gatun locks; and, as it was necessary to destroy both outer gate and inner guard gate, U-30 and U-31 each fired the four bow torpedoes in quick succession. To make sure of destroying the inner (guard) gates, we turned through 180 degrees so as to bring our stern tubes to bear, when each boat fired two more torpedoes.*

We then rose to the surface, coupled up engines, and drove ahead at 18 knots. As I approached Cristobal, saw several columns of water rise from the docks, indicating that U-31 was attacking the

* The Panama Canal being wrecked and incapable of operation, the pre-dreadnought fleet of the U. S. Navy was now separated by 14,000 miles of water from its main fleet.

enemy submarine flotilla of five boats. Passing the docks, I slowed down, and awaited U-32, which I presently saw returning full speed at the surface, having sunk the enemy as they lay moored at the dock. Rejoined light cruiser *Rostock*, whose commander informed me that, an hour before dawn, a landing party had surprised and captured the operating staff of the new long-distance radio plant at Colon, and after notifying Sayville Station in our cipher of the capture, had destroyed the electrical plant, and returned to the ship.

I have the honor to be,

Yours obediently,

W. NEUMANN, LIEUTENANT, I. G. N.

Report in cipher from long-distance naval radio station at Key West (captured), by way of Sayville Station (captured), to the Commander-in-Chief of the

German Expeditionary Fleet at New York:

> Light Cruiser, *Graudenz*,
>> Key West,
>>> April 1, 1916.

Commander-in-Chief, Imperial German Fleet, New York.

Surprise attack by landing party on Key West successful. Long-distance radio plant captured. Losses small, strong re-enforcements from transport now being landed. Submarine attack followed capture of radio.

Shall send message in the U. S. Navy secret code, to the commander-in-chief of the United States North Atlantic Fleet at Vera Cruz tomorrow.*

> LINK, CAPTAIN, I. G. N.

---

*The message sent by Captain Link was as follows: "Germany has declared war on the United States. Have information, German advance fleet is following southern course for Caribbean; second fleet on northern course for our Atlantic Coast.

Wireless report, via Sayville (captured), to the Admiralty, German Imperial Navy, Berlin.

Imperial German Expeditionary Fleet,
New York,
8 A.M., April 1, 1916.

ADMIRALTY, Berlin.

Favored by calm weather, our submarine attack, which took place in the dusk of early dawn, as planned, was everywhere successful. At Boston, New York, Norfolk, Charleston, Pensacola, and Cristobal, Panama, the surprise was so complete, that all enemy destroyers and submarines at those points were either sunk or completely dis-

Proceed full speed for Guantanamo Bay, Cuba, to take on coal and supplies. Find and destroy weaker advance German fleet. Send disabled ships to Hampton Roads, and proceed to Canal Zone, Panama. Under cover of guns of fortifications, await arrival of Third and Fourth Divisions of Atlantic Fleet from Pacific, and proceed north in full strength to engage second fleet of enemy."

abled. The gates at the Atlantic end of
the Gatun locks have been torpedoed, and
the Panama Canal put out of commission.
Information as to success at Panama
reached me from landing force at Colon,
which, after sending messages, destroyed
long-distance radio station there. Another landing force captured long-distance radio at Key West and sent
U. S. secret code message, directing U. S.
Atlantic fleet proceed Vera Cruz to Guantanamo. Information regarding success at
Boston, Norfolk, Charleston, and Pensacola was relayed to me by cruisers stationed
along coast for that purpose. Sayville Station captured early this A.M. by motorcycle
corps from landing force at New York.
My earlier report has given particulars of
the successful landing and operations of expeditionary force at this city. The situation is developing very favorably.

During voyage of fleet across Atlantic,

sighted only few ships, whose wireless was put out of commission by our destroyers with promise of full reparation.

> BUCHNER,
> *Commander-in-Chief,*
> *Imperial German Expeditionary Fleet.*

VIII

CAPTURE OF NEW YORK HARBOR DEFENCES

SHORTLY before midnight, March 31, 1916, a couple of destroyers, there being no moon, the sky overcast, and the night intensely dark, sped swiftly through the Ambrose Channel, and turning into the old Swash Channel, cut the cable connecting Sandy Hook with New York. While this was being done, a boat was sent ashore to cut the telegraph and telephone lines between Sandy Hook and Seabright. Soon afterwards two transports of moderate draught with all lights out, following the same course, headed in towards the Shrewsbury River as far as the depth of water would allow. The ships' boats,

loaded with troops, were already swung
out on the davits; and, within half an hour,
a force of 1,000 men was landed about
two miles below the fort and began its
silent march over the sandy neck of the
isthmus.   As it approached the buildings
at the southern extremity of the fort, the
force was divided, one half proceeding
along the beach. on the ocean side, the
other half advancing along the inner
beach.   At the time agreed upon, 1 : 30
A.M., the expedition closed in with a rush
upon the garrison, which, consisting of
only a few companies and barely awakened
by the shots of the sentries, was quickly
overpowered.   Before 2 A. M. Fort
Hancock was in the hands of the
enemy.

At 11 P.M. on the night of March 31st,
three large ships with lights out moved
quietly into deep water anchorage between
Far Rockaway inlet and the entrance to

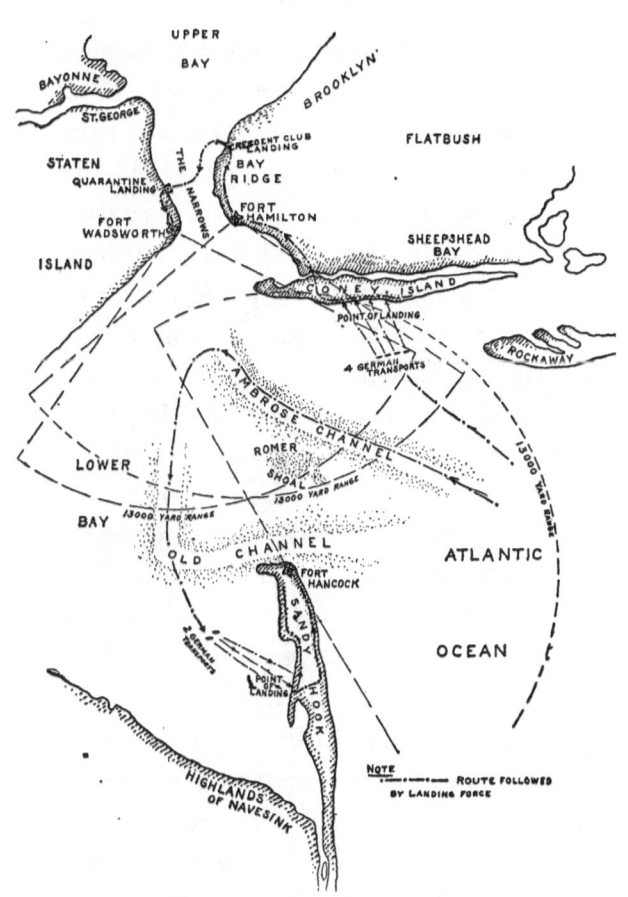

ROUTES FOLLOWED BY EXPEDITION IN THE CAPTURE OF
NEW YORK'S DEFENCES.

the Ambrose Channel. They were sur-
rounded by a cordon of destroyers. Had
any fisherman's boat been allowed to pass
the destroyers (which it was not), it
would have seen that all of the boats on
the transports were loaded with troops
and swung outboard ready for lowering.
The first boats to reach the water con-
tained detachments of expert linemen
and engineers of the German Imperial
Army. They were towed by a ship's
launch to the deserted beach, fronting the
Brighton Beach Hotel, and, mounting
their bicycles, they scattered and headed
for the country lying back of Coney
Island and the various beach resorts. The
linemen cut all the telegraph and telephone lines leading to Brooklyn and New
York; the engineers removed a rail from
every trolley and elevated track leading
to the city. Part of this detachment covered the highways leading from the Beach

and turned back all late-returning automobiles.

Meanwhile, under the cover of an impenetrable darkness, a force of 4,000 men was quietly landed in the ships' boats, which, in strings of half a dozen, were towed by steam launches to the beach and rowed ashore through the scarcely perceptible surf. The whole force had landed shortly after midnight. Drawn up in column of fours, it commenced a rapid march on Fort Hamilton, some six miles distant.

Realizing that there was a bare chance that no warning had reached its garrison of 600 men, the commander of the expedition hurried forward a bicycle detachment, 300 strong, for a surprise attack. The main body advanced by the road which skirts the shore of Gravesend Bay. When it was within three miles of the fort, the distant roll of musketry fire

showed that the garrison had been warned
and was offering a heavy resistance. Soon,
dispatch riders from the bicycle force
came back with the news that it had run
into a strong skirmish line, which the garrison had thrown out across the Bath
Beach road. The main body of troops
was now divided, a force of 1,000 being
sent across the Fort Hamilton road with
orders to advance from the north as soon
as the main attack was pressed home from
the south.

Despite the heroic resistance of the garrison, during which our regulars lived up
to the finest traditions of the United
States Army, the final rush of the German
veterans could not be denied, and by 3 :00
A.M. Fort Hamilton was in the hands of
the enemy.

Leaving half of his force to hold the
fort and entrench the position on the land
side, the commander of the expedition,

with 1,800 men, marched north by the shore road in the direction of Bay Ridge.

Between two and three on the morning of April 1st, a strange thing happened aboard the Staten Island ferryboat as it was about to leave its landing at the Battery. No sooner had the last passenger for Manhattan stepped ashore than the gates were closed, and two men entered the pilot house, covered the captain with their revolvers, and ordered him instantly to pull out from the dock and head for Staten Island.

"What are you fellows after, anyway?" asked the captain. "Money?"

"Not at all. We are officers of the German Naval Reserve. War has been declared by Germany against the United States; Forts Hancock and Hamilton are already in our possession; and," with a smile, "by your kind permission we shall make use of your boat to transfer troops

for the capture of Fort Wadsworth. You
will be so good as to hand the wheel over
to me and take that chair, making yourself as comfortable in mind and body as
the exigencies of the present situation will
allow."

Commander Schultz, I. G. N., took the
wheel and headed the big ferryboat for the
Narrows. At the entrance he swung to
port, and made for the dock of the Cres-
cent Athletic Club, on the Brooklyn side.
Not long thereafter was heard the tramp
of marching men on the shore road, leading from Fort Hamilton, and in ten minutes' time the big ferryboat had backed
away from the pier with 1,800 men
aboard. The boat crossed the Narrows,
and, the tide being at the flood, was enabled to push her nose up to the quaran-
tine landing at Staten Island. But no
sooner was she made fast than the shore
line flashed with the rifle fire of the Wads-

worth garrison, which had thrown out scouting parties in all directions in anticipation of attack.

The ferryboat backed quickly into midstream, while a flotilla of German destroyers searched the shore with a storm of projectiles from their rapid-fire and machine-guns. Under cover of this the debarkation was effected. The German force, 1,800 strong, deployed and moved on the fort. Its garrison, consisting of only 400 men, fought it out stubbornly from building to building; but against such odds the result was inevitable, and by 4:30 A.M. the last of the great defensive works of New York Harbor was captured.

And thus it came about that by daybreak of April 1st the mighty seacoast guns and the elaborate system of mortar batteries, which constitute the defences of New York, being utterly unprotected in the rear, fell into the hands of the enemy.

IX

INDEMNITY OR BOMBARDMENT

WITH the coming of the dawn of April
1st, the mantle of clouds which had helped
to obscure the fateful events of the night
broke and scattered before a fresh wind
out of the northwest. Over sea and land
and city the sun shone brilliantly in that
crystal-clear atmosphere, which is the sure
accompaniment of a northwest breeze.

And as the sun came up, there lifted
over the eastern horizon the van of a
stately column of warships—the dreadnought fleet of the Imperial German Navy.
Into the Ambrose Channel they headed,
led by the *Koenig,* flagship of Admiral
Buchner, commander-in-chief of the German expeditionary fleet. Well off shore,
the Admiral had waited through the

night for the wireless message, telling him that the capture of the defences of New York had opened a safe passage for his fleet into the upper bay. The message came, as he knew it must, in due course; and immediately signal was made for the fleet to steam at full speed for the harbor entrance.

Following the flagship, in single column, were the dreadnoughts of the *Koenig* and *Kaiser* classes, making, with the *Koenig*, nine in all; a division of armored cruisers, headed by the *Roon;* and a division of light cruisers.

Thrown out fanwise in the van of the fleet and flanking it on each side in two parallel columns were the destroyer flotillas.

When that stately line had swept through the Narrows, signal was made for half speed; and after hugging the easterly side of the Channel, the flagship of each division of dreadnoughts turned eight points to port and the fleet anchored. They lay bow and stern, in two parallel columns, 2,000 yards apart, with the starboard batteries bearing on the city of New York.

Every ship was cleared for action; and on each the battle-flags were flying.

Meanwhile on shore the engineer companies of the German troops in Forts Hancock, Hamilton, and Wadsworth, after selecting the points of vantage for defence of the landward approaches, had staked out the trenches, and the Germans were feverishly digging and fortifying against attack. The 3-inch rapid-fire guns for protecting the mine fields were unbolted from their concrete foundations, and remounted in selected positions on hastily-improvised platforms. Also, the 3-inch landing guns of the fleet were brought ashore in the ships' boats and wheeled into position.

The garrisons were strengthened by a force of 2,000 marines, landed from the fleet.

In short, within a few hours of occupation, the enemy had provided our coast fortifications with those organized defences, on the land side, which, had Congress given heed to the recommendations of its military advisers, would have long ago been completed and would have served to hold the enemy at bay until reenforcements could have been brought up in sufficient strength to drive him back to the sea.

Scarcely had the flagship of Admiral Buchner dropped her anchor, than a launch, flying a white flag, left the ship, steamed up the harbor, and landed at the Battery. Captain Dornfeld of the Admiral's staff stepped ashore, strode through the Park to a waiting automobile, and with a slight nod of recognition to the chauf-

feur, took his seat, and was driven swiftly
to the City Hall. It was early for an
official call (9 A.M.), but the emissary
guessed rightly that the Mayor would be
in his off.ce. His name and mission gained
him instant audience.

Five minutes later a call went out from
the Mayor's office, requesting the instant
attendance of the heads of New York's
great banking houses and financial institutions.

When that distinguished company had
gathered the Mayor said: " Gentlemen,
it is my painful duty to announce to you—
if indeed you are not aware of it already
—that the fortifications protecting the approaches to New York are in the hands of
a German expeditionary force, which, by
a surprise attack (following a declaration
of war by Germany, that reached the Secretary of State, at Washington, early this
morning), has obtained full possession.

A fleet of the enemy's dreadnoughts, nine
in number, has entered and is now covering the city with its guns.

" I hold in my hands an ultimatum from
the Commander-in-Chief of the fleet,
which I will read to you:

Imperial German Expeditionary Fleet,
    Upper Bay, New York Harbor,
                    April 1, 1916.
To His Honor the Mayor of
    New York.

Sir:—I have the honor to inform you
that the German Government having declared war on the United States, a force
was landed and, early this morning, captured all the fortifications covering the
approaches to New York.

The fleet under my command, consisting
of nine of the latest and most powerful
dreadnoughts of the German Imperial
Navy, is now anchored in the upper bay.

The heavy guns of the fleet, ninety in all, with an extreme range of fifteen miles, command practically the whole of Greater New York.

I am instructed by my Government to demand of you a ransom of five billion dollars, the bond for which, together with a first payment of five hundred million dollars in gold, must be delivered on board the flagship, twenty-four hours after the delivery of this ultimatum, that is to say, by 9 A.M. on April 2d. Failing the receipt of this at or before the hour named I shall open fire on your city.

If, during the twenty-four hours covered by the truce, any movement of troops, either of the regular army or of the National Guard, takes place, I shall immediately commence bombardment.

I have the honor to be

BUCHNER,
Commander-in-Chief.

At the request of the Mayor, Captain Dornfeld, bearer of the ultimatum, withdrew to the anteroom.

The first to speak was the Comptroller, who said: " Obviously the thing to be done is to ascertain what are the facts of the military and naval situation. We should send a request to Governor's Island for the immediate attendance here of the Commander of the Department of the East."

" That I have already done," said the Mayor. " He was to return to-day from a tour of inspection, and my secretary has by this time, doubtless, met him. He should be with us in a few minutes. Meanwhile, gentlemen, what are you prepared to do in this emergency ? "

" I am satisfied," said one of the Mayor's invited guests, who was famous alike as a pacificist and philanthropist, " that this whole thing is a colossal April fool's joke. It is so preposterous, in fact, that it appeals to my Scotch sense of the humorous—or the canny—I scarce know which. Five bil—— Why, that is just five times as much as my late friend Bismarck demanded of the whole French nation, to liquidate the cost of the war of 1870.

"Five billions, and immediate payment in gold of five hundred millions! I cannot believe, gentlemen, that this outrageous descent upon the shores of a friendly nation is made with the consent of the great German people, or by command of my friend the Kaiser. Why, I well remember that in the course of an intimate talk with him at Pots——"

But this interesting personal reminiscence was interrupted by the entrance of Major-General Adams, to whom the Mayor handed the ultimatum, without a word.

After he had read the fateful document the Mayor said: " General, we have asked you to come here to tell us what are the military and naval conditions, and what the city can do to escape this dilemma ? "

" Mr. Mayor, the conditions are exactly as stated in this paper, and New York City can do—nothing! The country is confronted with a catastrophe for which the indifference and neglect of the people and its Congress are entirely to blame. That the naval and military defences of the United States were totally inadequate has been known to naval and military men for a generation past. Year after year the General Staff and the General Board of the Navy have warned the nation that its unpreparedness was such that this very disaster, which has now fallen upon us like a thunderbolt, might come at any hour.

" Briefly, let me tell you the conditions:

Your land defences are in the hands of the
enemy, our battleships are at Vera Cruz,
and the lesser units of the Navy, and particularly the destroyers and submarines,
were sunk in our navy yards at daybreak.
The German fleet, freed from any menace
from forts, submarines, destroyers, or our
own battleship fleet, is in a position absolutely to destroy New York and take its
own time to do it. Our few scattered
regulars in the vicinity are concentrating
and the National Guard is assembling at
its armories. They might in time recapture
the forts—though even this is doubtful;
for I learn that fresh transports are arriv-
ing every hour and the landing of reënforcements is proceeding. Moreover, ac-
cording to this ultimatum, any further concentration of our troops will bring on the
bombardment.

"Mr. Mayor, if you wish to save the
city, whose total value, I believe, Mr.

Comptroller, is twenty billion dollars, there is but one possible way to do it, and that is for you gentlemen to devise at once the ways and means for a cash payment in gold of five hundred million dollars and a guarantee of the balance of the five billion dollars demanded."

The General left the room. With his departure the spirit of optimism began to prevail and ultimately a committee was appointed which decided to make a counter proposal of one billion, with a cash payment of fifty millions in gold. Meanwhile the Federal Government gave orders that no military demonstration should be made for the next twenty-four hours.

This proposal was handed to Captain Dornfeld, who promptly returned to the flagship.

The afternoon and evening wore away; but no answer came from the German

Admiral. "He is communicating with
Berlin," said the committee; "we shall
hear in the morning."

And they did—from the throats of a
hundred guns!

X

THE BOMBARDMENT OF NEW YORK

FROM his point of vantage, over 700 feet in midair, Kennedy, the attendant on the observation platform of the tower of the Woolworth Building, might have swept his eye over the grandest panoramic view of a great city that it has ever been granted to mortal eye to look upon. But on that particular day, April 2d, and at that particular hour, 9 A.M., he gazed neither east, north, nor west. His face was to the south, and his eye riveted upon a group of dark-gray ships that stretched in two parallel lines across the main ship channel of the Upper Bay, somewhat to the north of Robbin's Reef—the German dreadnoughts!

He had read in the papers of the night

before about that absurd demand for five
billion dollars, and from the papers, also,
he knew that the city had made a counter
proposal of one billion. The morning ex-
tras had told him that no reply had come
from the German Admiral, " who, doubtless, was awaiting instructions from Berlin." He picked up a pair of field glasses
(an investment of his which had long ago
paid for itself, and was now a steady
source of income in tips from country
visitors to the tower) and sought out the
flagship. Yes, there she was at the head
of the first line, with the Admiral's flag flying at the—but what was that flash, keen
as the flash of a mirror in the sun! Could
it be that—and there came a crash, louder
than that of any thunderbolt from heaven,
and he was clutching wildly at the railing,
as the whole mass of the tower shuddered,
and then swayed for a few seconds like a
reed shaken by the wind.

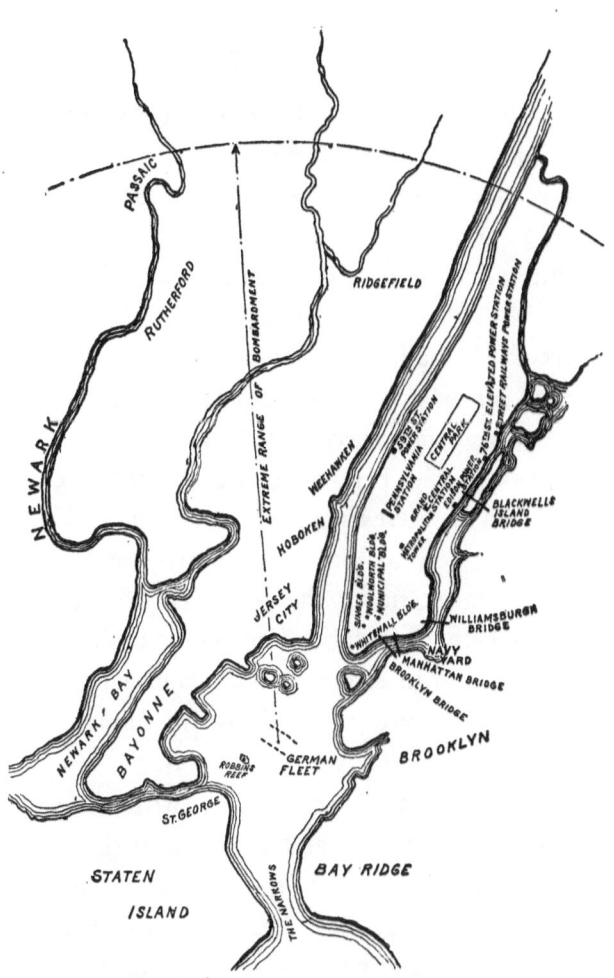

MAP SHOWING HOW GUNS OF GERMAN FLEET COVERED
THE WHOLE OF MANHATTAN.

Driven by the instinct of flight, he rushed around the platform to the north side, and, looking down, saw that the buildings were obscured by a cloud of bricks, dust, and broken terra cotta, which fell with a prolonged roar, like a fall of Cyclopean hail, upon the roofs and pavement far below. Another crash! Again the tower staggered under the blow!

He jumped for the elevator. Yes, it was intact. A few floors down it stopped. He managed to undo the door, crawled out, and ran down the stairway. Three flights below he stood dumfounded. The stairs ended in space, and through a gaping hole, where the hollow-tile flooring had been blasted entirely away, he saw that the whole of two stories, with their floors, outer walls, and inside partitions, had been blown clear into space, leaving the skeleton of the building—columns, floor beams, and braces—stripped as clean

of its brick and terra-cotta walls as it was
when the erecting gang had swung it into
place, a few years before.

The stairs were gone; the elevator
shafts also. There was nothing for him
but to return. If he could not go down, he
would go up. Odd to relate, fear was
giving place to curiosity. He heard the
roar of the 12-inch shells, as they hurtled
past the tower to fall upon the doomed
city, and the observation platform would
enable him to watch the stupendous spec-
tacle of its destruction.

He gained the platform just in time to
see two shells, in quick succession, pass
through the top stories of the towering
Equitable Life Building, and blast two
gaping holes in the south wall.

The next mark was the beautiful tower
that crowned the Municipal Building.
The percussion fuses were functioning
with deadly precision; nothing wrong with

these German shells. Just one hit—and
the walls and columns of the tower had
been tumbled in a confused mass upon the
roof of the main building and into the
street below, leaving the twisted steel
skeleton stripped as bare as the trees in
midwinter.

And now it dawned upon Kennedy that
the Germans were shooting up the city
upon a predetermined plan, picking out the
principal buildings and putting a couple
of shots into the upper stories of each. In
rapid succession the Singer Tower, the
City Investing Building, the Adams Express, and the new Western Union Buildings were struck; and always the gaping
holes were blown out hundreds of feet in
midair, where the ruin was visible to the
surging mass of people that swarmed out,
like bees from a hive, into the streets
below.

And then the din of the alternating

boom of guns and crash of bursting shells
ceased as suddenly as it began. Kennedy
turned his glasses on the fleet and saw a
couple of hydro-aëroplanes lifted by
cranes from the deck of an auxiliary ship
and placed in the water. They rose as
they advanced on the city, over which they
flew at an altitude of 1,500 feet. One of
them swung off at the Battery and began
to fly in a circular path. The other passed
on until it reached the Fifty-ninth Street
power station of the Subway, above which
it began to describe a path of the figure
eight. Kennedy turned his glasses upon
the fleet. One of the guns in No. 1 turret of the flagship was being slowly elevated until it pointed well into the sky.
There was a flash—a long, droning hum—
and thirty seconds later he saw the shell
burst against a building north of the power
station. From the hydro-aëroplane above
there was dropped a puff of white smoke.

Another flash and this time the shell
burst somewhat to the south of the station.
There followed two more puffs of smoke
from the 'plane. A few minutes later
every 12-inch gun on the ship rose to the
range and flashed forth its 860-pound shell
loaded with deadly explosive. Kennedy
heard the salvo go roaring by miles up in
the air, and, lo! the walls of the great
power station seemed to fall asunder and
a huge cloud of smoke and dust rose high
in the heavens.

The power station was utterly wrecked,
and every train in the Subway from the
Bronx to Brooklyn stopped with its terror-
stricken passengers in a darkness which
could be felt!

Then the aviator sailed northeast and
began his fateful maneuvers above the
Seventy-sixth Street power station of the
Elevated Railways. The same routine
followed: two or three ranging shots; the

dropping of smoke signals, which were relayed by the 'plane at the Battery to the ship; and, finally, the salvo. In a few minutes every train on the Elevated was out of commission.

North the aviator now sped, until he was hovering like a remorseless fate above the Ninety-first Street power station, which runs the street-railway system of Manhattan. The relay hydro-aëroplane moved up to First Street. In ten minutes' time a salvo had found its mark, and Manhattan was absolutely bereft of all means of transportation.

. . . .

That hive of busy workers known as "the downtown district" received its quota of the morning "rush" earlier than usual on April 2d. The optimistic tone assumed by the New York press was reflected among the citizens, who were sat-

isfied that there would be at least a period
of negotiations preceding any bombardment, the result of which, it was not
doubted, would be a compromise. It was
curiosity which filled up the business offices
half an hour earlier than usual—and
curiosity it was that carried the employees
by thousands to the roofs for a look at the
Kaiser's dreadnoughts.

But when that first 12-inch shell flashed
from the flagship, and went roaring over-
head across the skies to burst in the Woolworth Tower, curiosity gave place to fear
and fear to panic. From the roof to the
floors below the fleeing crowd of clerks
and stenographers ran, shouting that the
Germans were bombarding the city. Every
office floor disgorged its occupants, and a
growing crowd rushed for the elevators
and filled the stairways. Out of the entrance of every building there surged a human flood, and the waters of this inunda-

tion met and swirled in the side streets and turned in increasing volume to Broadway—seeking a means of quick escape by the Subway. In a few minutes the streets were filled from building line to building line with a frantic mob, so tightly jammed that all movement ceased. Then, as shell after shell burst far above, huge masses of masonry came hurtling down upon that hapless mob, killing and wounding the unfortunates where they stood, held fast. And still the terror-stricken pushed their way, with that fatal accumulation of pressure which marks a fleeing mob, out of every office-building entrance; the emerging mass acting with the cumulative effect of a hydraulic ram upon the already compacted mass in the streets. Under that fatal pressure the weak went down, ribs were crushed in, breathing was no longer possible. By the hundred, the people died where they fell.

And up from the streets of the city there rose the prolonged wail of the dying, answered from above by the savage roar of the flying shells, and the swish and clatter of the ever-falling masonry.

There was a slight relief at each Subway entrance, into which the waters of that stricken human flood twisted and gurgled like water through a sink. And further relief was given on the outskirts of the mob, where such of the police as had not been engulfed, attacking from the side streets, unloosened the fringe of the horror, by reminding the terror-stricken that the Elevated and the ferries afforded other avenues of escape.

And then, as the great power stations fell beneath the salvos of the bombardment, and every wheel in New York's vast system of transportation ceased to turn, fear redoubled and frantic horror began again to crush the life out of that hope-abandoned mob.

And just at this very hour, as though the anguish were not complete, the lawless element in the city broke loose in every quarter in a wild orgie of pillage and arson. From many a resort of crime and infamy, the gunman, the safe-cracker, and all the brood that hides from law and order streamed forth to gather in the spoil. The police, aye the whole ten thousand of them, swept off their feet by the wild terror of Manhattan's millions, were unable to co-operate for effective work. Crime had found its millennium. Into the jewelry stores, into the houses of the rich on Fifth Avenue and the West Side, a mob, armed and stopping at no crime of violence, broke its way, gathering into grip and handbag, or thrusting into pocket at each grasp, the ransom of a prince!

The terror of the bombardment swept

through the densely populated tenement-
house district like the rush of a prairie
fire, and at once there arose in a babel of
many tongues the universal cry: " To the
bridges; to the bridges!" And to the
bridges they swept, men, women, and chil-
dren, Jew, Italian, Greek, and Russian,
bearded rabbi and toddling child, in a
wild stampede to put the river between
themselves and the bursting shells. Eastward to the bridges they surged, half a
million strong; the mob becoming denser
as it converged on the various approaches.

Overwhelmed by that human flood,
vehicular traffic stopped. Roadways and
footways, subway tracks and trolley tracks,
all were submerged. The Manhattan
Bridge, among others, in spite of its width
of 120 feet, was packed from rail to rail
with the fleeing host, and when the crush
was at its worst the inevitable happened.
Somewhere a fugitive slipped, a foot pass-

ing between the railroad ties of the tracks
—someone stayed to help—more stum-
bled and fell. The crowd behind, in-
furiated by the delay, made a rush, throwing down others in the van. Soon, there
was a mass of struggling, cursing humanity wedged tight from rail to rail, prevent-
ing down others in the van. Soon there
thousand behind stayed not their rush.
The crushing out of life that was happening on lower Broadway was being repeated
150 feet above the East River.

And just then there sailed above the
bridge, high in air, a German hydro-
aëroplane. The mob saw it and knew the
meaning of the dread portent. " God in
Heaven, they are going to shell the
bridge!" And then the strange thing happened. The crowd stopped its convulsive
struggle. Except for the down-trodden
and dying, silence fell on that multitude,
and, awestruck, they gazed skyward at the

harbinger of death and waited for his messengers.

Then they came. A roar as of an express train on the Elevated, and with a blast of air that swept down upon the victims, a 12-inch shell passed over the center of the span.

But before signaling to correct the range, the aviator planed down so as to obtain a closer view of the bridge. With amazement he saw that it was swarming from end to end with a helpless mass of humanity. The purpose of the bombardment was to damage—not destroy; and he realized that if the shells of the *Koenig* should cut the bridge cables, 50,000 souls would be hurled to their death in the river below!

Hastily he rose and signaled to the *Koenig* to cease fire.

XI

THE CAPITULATION OF NEW YORK

IN response to the call of the Mayor, the Committee representing the financial institutions of the City met in his office promptly at 9 A.M. on April 2d. A member was proposing that a wireless message be dispatched to the German Admiral, requesting an early answer to the Committee's proposal of the day before, when the boom of a heavy explosion shook the building, and the Mayor, looking up through the southwest window, quietly remarked, "Gentlemen, the answer has come!" The Committee turned and saw in the fair white northern face of the beautiful Woolworth Tower a yawning cavity —and, filling the air below, a mass of falling débris!

117

The crisis had come, swift and appalling; and with a steady nerve and a quick-thinking brain each man of that Committee set himself to meet it. There was much to do, and it must be done quickly. First, as to that cash payment of half a billion in gold. Was there that much gold in the city? The question was quickly answered. In the sub-treasury was one hundred and twenty million dollars; in the banks and other depositories, four hundred and fifty million dollars, more or less. Yes, the cash payment could be made— that very day, if demanded. And, as for the other four-and-a-half billions,—well, New York, even with that financial burden to carry, was better than a New York thrown down by bombardment and ravaged by a universal conflagration.

And so, while the cannon thundered and the fleeing citizens surged past the City Hall, seeking a way of escape by Subway,

Elevated, or Bridge, those men seated in
the private office of the Mayor worked
out a plan for the salvation of the city.

At 10 A.M. a wireless message was
sent to the fleet anouncing the capitulation
of the city and the start of the Mayor, the
Comptroller, and Committee to confer
with the Admiral on board the *Koenig*.

Guarded by a cordon of police, who
with difficulty had fought their way to the
City Hall, the Mayor and Committee were
escorted to the foot of Spruce Street on the
East River, where they boarded the patrol
boat of the Police Department and
steamed out to the Upper Bay.

The roar of the bombardment had
ceased, and save for a few shell holes in
the taller buildings, there was nothing
to indicate that, for one fell hour, Hell
had vented its fury upon their noble city.

Arrived at the gangway of the *Koenig*,
the Mayor and his Committee were re-

ceived by the executive officer with every
mark of distinction, and escorted to the
Admiral's quarters.

He was tall, blond, blue-eyed, affable,
and supremely ceremonious. Moreover,
he spoke most excellent English.

"He was sensible," he said, "of the
great honor conferred upon the German
Navy, upon the flagship, and upon himself,
by the presence on board of the Mayor of
the great commercial metropolis of the
Western Hemisphere, attended by so
many representatives of its leading financial houses.

"He could have wished that this meeting had taken place under less distressing
circumstances; but—well—war is war, and
upon him, as one under authority, had
fallen the unhappy duty of bringing their
city to terms by force of arms."

Picking up a document from his table
he said: "The conditions on which I am

instructed to cease all further naval attack on New York are as follows:

" I. The payment by the City of New
York of an indemnity of five billion
dollars.

" II. The payment of the first install-
ment to be made in the form of five hundred million dollars in gold, the same to be
delivered within twenty-four hours of the
signing of this agreement.

" III. The surrender of the Custom
House, New York, and its occupation by
German forces until the payment of the
balance of the indemnity has been completed.

" IV. The surrender of the Chelsea
steamship piers for the use of the German
troopships.

" V. The surrender of all armories in
New York and Brooklyn for the use of the
troops of the German Expeditionary
Force.

" It is my wish, Mr. Mayor, that, for the present, at least, you continue to exercise full civil control of New York, under the rules of military occupation of my government."

After very brief conference the articles of capitulation were duly signed, and shortly thereafter the Police Department launch cast off from the gangway of the *Koenig* and headed for Manhattan.

Silent and preoccupied, the group of men on her upper deck gazed wistfully upon the stately buildings of lower Manhattan, which lifted their shell-scarred summits far into the blue of that sunlit April day.

" Well," said one of the party, " such are the caprices of Fortune."

"Nay, sir," sharply retorted the Mayor, " say rather that such are the fruits of folly and criminal neglect! "

.   .   .   .

That afternoon, closed and heavily guarded motor vans began to make their way from the banks of New York City to a German transport at Pier No. 1, the Battery; and before noon of the day following five hundred million dollars, or about 1,000 tons, in gold, had been put aboard, and the vessel, under heavy naval escort, had sailed for a German port.

XII

THE combined sea and land expedition for
the capture of Boston by a surprise attack
consisted of a division of dreadnoughts,
some destroyers, a flotilla of six submarines, and a landing force of 5,000
picked veterans of the European war.

The defences of Boston consisted of
seven forts. Two of these, Fort Heath
and Fort Banks, were built on the eastern
shore of the peninsula which incloses Boston Harbor on the north. The others
were advantageously placed on five of the
islands which cover the approaches to the
harbor. Three of these, Forts Standish,
Warren, and Revere, formed the outer line
of defence; the inner line consisted of Forts
Strong and Andrews. They were heavily

armed with 10- and 12-inch rifles—the lat-
ter having an extreme range of 13,000
yards. There were also some 12-inch
mortar batteries of approximately the same
range.

Although the range exceeded the effective fighting range of any existing battleships at the time the forts were built, it was
far short of the range of naval guns in the
year 1916. Moreover, the Boston forts,
like those defending New York, were open
to attack from the rear. All of the guns
and mortars pointed seaward. Further-
more, thanks to the parsimony of Congress,
the whole of these defences were under-
manned, there being only 1,100 men distributed among the seven forts.

The expedition timed its approach so
as to be within a few hours' steaming of
the Massachusetts coast at sundown, March
31, where it divided, the four transports
carrying 5,000 men making for Salem,

and the warships moving on Boston. The submarines, having filled their fuel tanks from the tender, pushed forward until they reached the outer defences, when they submerged and, under cover of the dark, worked their way carefully through the channels, reaching Boston Navy Yard in the early dawn. Here, at 4:30 A.M., they torpedoed and sunk every ship in the yard, sending to the bottom the armored cruiser *Brooklyn*, the scout cruisers *Chester* and *Salem*, the cruiser *Chicago*, the gunboat *Castine*, and two or three smaller units. The submarines then submerged to the bottom and went to sleep, awaiting developments.

The transports, favored by an unusually dark night, there being no moon, reached Salem undetected. Debarkation commenced at 2 A.M. The first troops to be landed consisted of a bicycle corps, 1,500 strong, which immediately made a dash for

Boston, twelve miles distant. Five hundred of these followed the shore road, and
at 4 A.M. rushed the garrison, 200 strong,
of Forts Heath and Banks, which they took
in reverse. The rest of the force, 1,000
strong, entered Boston, one half capturing
the Navy Yard, while the other, crossing
the Charles River, seized the large motor
fishing boats and other motor craft at the
docks and took them over to the Navy
Yard.

Meanwhile the debarkation of the balance of the expeditionary force, 3,500
strong, was being effected. The troops
landed in light marching order, with two
days' rations in their knapsacks, and ac-
companied by strong batteries of machine-
guns. By daylight the column was on the
march, and at 8 A.M., after a sharp engagement in the suburbs, and almost within
sight of Bunker Hill, with such of the
militia as it was possible hastily to assem-

ble, the enemy moved into the Navy Yard and began to embark on the miscellaneous craft which had been gathered there.

Meanwhile the German dreadnoughts had moved in on the outer line of seacoast defences. They anchored at a distance of 17,000 yards, or between 2,000 and 3,000 yards beyond the extreme range to which the guns of the forts could carry. Accompanying the fleet was an aëroplane tender, and by the time the ships were ready to open fire three aëroplanes were circling above the outer forts—Standish, Warren, and Revere.

The calm sea and clear weather which favored the operations of April 1st along the Atlantic Coast prevailed at Boston. Vision was exceptionally good, and the German gunners, being outside the range of the forts and quite unmolested, and being guided by aëroplane observation, quickly got on the target, and placed their

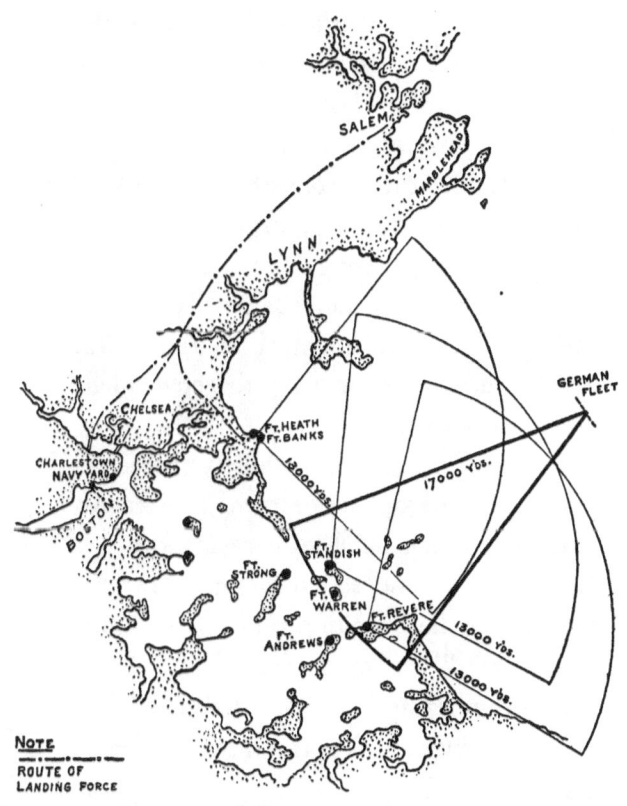

MAP SHOWING HOW GERMANS BOMBARDED BOSTON FORT
FROM A POSITION OUTSIDE THE RANGE
OF THEIR GUNS.

high explosive 11-inch shells with deadly accuracy. After half an hour of bombardment a division of destroyers was sent in to draw the fire of the forts by steaming swiftly across their front at 10,000 yards' range. There was a vigorous reply from Forts Warren, Strong, and Andrews, but the fire from Forts Standish and Revere was feeble. The bombardment continued for another hour, the fire being directed chiefly at the inner forts.

It was now 9 A.M. and shortly thereafter one of the aëroplanes returned to report that the motor-boat fleet, carrying the land forces, had been descried moving down the bay to take the forts in reverse. The signal " cease fire " was made from the flagship, and the garrisons, already decimated and shaken up by shell fire, faced about to meet the new attack.

The motor-boat fleet moved upon the inner forts (Strong and Andrews) in two

parallel columns, flanked on each wing by
three submarines, which, moving awash,
had broken out the 3-inch guns with which
they were armed. Under the cover of these
guns, which swept the landing with a storm
of shells, the German troops were landed,
and the garrison, consisting in each case of
only four companies, after a spirited resistance, was forced to surrender. The expedition then moved on the three outer
forts, and as there was only a single
company in each, and half of these
had been killed or wounded by the
bombardment, they offered little or no
resistance.

As soon as the Admiral saw the German
flag flying over the forts, he moved into a
position from which he could cover the
whole of Boston with his guns. A launch,
bearing a flag of truce, left the flagship,
and within half an hour the city was confronted with an ultimatum, demanding the

payment of three billion dollars, two hundred millions of which was to be delivered
aboard ship within twenty-four hours. The
custom house and the armories were to be
occupied immediately by German troops.
The Mayor was to remain in civil control,
under the rules of German military occupation. Finally, the ultimatum stated that if
any movement of the regular or militia
forces, having in view the recapture of Boston, took place, the fleet would open on the
city with all its guns.

The Mayor called a meeting of the leading bankers and an effort was made to obtain a mitigation of the terms. The truce
was to expire at 2 P.M., April 2d; but on
learning that the bombardment of New
York had begun, the city at once capit-
ulated.

That night one of the transports was
sent round from Salem, and by noon of
April 3d she had sailed for a German port

with two hundred million dollars in her
hold.

.   .   .   .   .

On the afternoon of April 2d two German armored cruisers and two light cruisers arrived at Boston from New York, and
that evening the German Admiral, leaving
these ships, some destroyers, and the submarines to cover the city, sailed with his
division of dreadnoughts for New York.

On the evening of April 3d the dreadnought fleet of Admiral Buchner put to sea
and picked up the division from Boston,
and the fleet of thirteen dreadnoughts
sailed for the Caribbean.

XIII

THE CAPTURE OF WASHINGTON

At intervals during the morning of March
31st four large German merchant ships,
duly consigned to Baltimore for the avowed
purpose of rushing to that port certain orders for German goods which had been
delayed by the war, passed in through the
Capes, reported to the signal station, and
proceeded up the Chesapeake. In the upper
reaches of the Bay, after sundown, they
closed up; and about midnight they anchored well away from the course followed
by shipping, and abreast a fine stretch of
sandy beach which lines the western shore
of the Bay, a few miles below Annapolis.
The sky was clouded and the night intensely
dark.

Two hours before midnight commenced

the debarkation from these ships of a force
of 5,000 picked bicycle troops. Accompanying them were several batteries of
machine-guns, bicycle-mounted and capable
of being quickly assembled. The first company to land was told off to cut all telegraph, telephone, and railway lines leading
to Washington. A small detachment from
this company, composed of fast riders,—
more than one of whom, in past years, had
come over for the international races in
Madison Square,—pushed on at full speed
for Washington, with instructions to mine
the tall towers of the Arlington long-distance radio station, lay the wires, and be
prepared to wreck the plant as soon as the
expeditionary force reached the city.

Except for the machine-guns (each of
which was carried between a pair of tan-
dems) the whole force was in the lightest
possible marching order, each man carrying
only two days' rations and an extra supply

of ammunition. As soon as the troops
landed, lamps were lit and they moved off
silently into the night. By 2:30 A.M. the
whole expedition was ashore. Just before
daybreak the bulk of the raiding force,
assembled on several roads leading into
Washington, made its rush for the capture
of the city.

Carefully planned though it was, the surprise was not complete. Willard Bronson,
a correspondent recently returned from
service at the front with the German army,
had run out on his motorcycle on the evening of March 31st, to visit an old friend
who lived some fifteen miles, or halfway
from Washington, on the Annapolis road.
There was much to tell; and it was between 2 and 3 A.M. when he left the
house and brought his machine around
from the stable. He was just about to
light up, when he paused, match in hand,
as the glare of a hundred lights shone

down the road, and the van of the raiding force swept noiselessly by on the other
side of the heavy privet hedge separating
the lawn from the road.

"German mounted bicycle troops! Impossible; absurd!" But Bronson had been
trained to clear thinking and quick action.
There flashed into his mind the startling
headlines of the afternoon papers, announc-
ing the purchase of St. Thomas.

But this would be war before war was
declared. True; yet there was the prece-
dent of Japan's attack on Port Arthur.

Bronson slipped quietly back to the house
and burst in upon his astonished host:
"Quick, tell me, is there any road by which
I can cut around into the main road—any
path, cattle-track, anything on which a
wheel can turn? Don't stare at me like
that, man! Here, come to the window—see
those lights sweeping by? It is the German
army moving on Washington. I must warn

them—the Government—or they will make
a bag of the whole Cabinet before dawn!"

"Yes; two fields away—good grassland
—you can ride—there is a country road
which intersects the main road two miles
from here; but you must ride like the very
devil!"

With lamp alight he swept across the
first field—good; the gate was open. The
gate to the road was shut—cruel delay,
with the fate of a nation hanging on the
chance of a minute!

Again he swung into the saddle, and,
thank God, the searchlight beam of his
lamp showed, straight and fair, a smooth,
though grass-grown, lane. Wide went the
throttle, and, ah! how he would have liked
to open the muffler too. Thirty, forty, fifty
miles an hour. The road swung gently
away to the left. Now it swung back
again, and there, abreast of him, through
the trees and across the fields, he could see

the head of the raiding column. The lane
and the road were convergent. And now
he noticed that the leading lights were
stringing out. He was discovered; the
purr of his motor and the gleam of his
lamp had been noted, and they were sprint-
ing to head him off. Open went his muffler,
and, head down, he, the modern Paul
Revere, swept into the main road, just one
hundred yards ahead of the leading troops.
With brake hard down and machine skid-
ding over to the further ditch, fortune favored his desperate dash, and he straightened out for Washington.

Behind, he heard the clash of falling bicycles. " Ah! they have jumped from their
machines to take a long shot "—and above
the roar of his motor he heard the crackle
of rifle fire. Zip, zip, zip, the bullets sang.
" I am going a good mile a minute now—
they'll never get me—Oh, H——! " Like
a blow from a baseball bat it struck him—

right leg—in the calf. "Too bad—but I
can see the lights of Washington—only a
few minutes, and I shall be at the telephone exchange. God, how it stings!"
He reached down and his hand felt the
gush of the warm blood.

.   .   .   .

The routine of work for the night force
at the central telephone exchange at Washington, D. C., was suddenly broken at 3:30
A.M., April 1st, when the door was labori-
ously opened and a man, on all fours,
crawled into the room, dragging after him
a broken leg that left a smear of blood on
the floor. Propping himself on his hands,
he raised his face, white and twitching, and
shouted in a burst of staccato sentences:
" The Germans are coming—landed at Annapolis—here in half hour—warn members
of Cabinet escape Union Station—tell
garage send taxis each house—quick, quick,

for the love of our country—the President first, then the——"

And with a groan he crumpled up and lay as though dead before the gaping night force.

Then the spell broke—they rushed to the fallen man. "Why, it's Bronson, the war correspondent," said Murphy, "and if Bronson says the Germans are coming, coming they are. For God's sake get busy."

And they did so to such good effect that, as the enemy swept into the city in the early dawn, there pulled out of the Union Station, for Philadelphia, an express train, bearing the members of the Cabinet and their families, together with the ranking official in the Departments of War, the Navy, and Finance.

The seizure of the city was accomplished with characteristic precision and dispatch. Every company and detachment had its objective. The advance force, 1,200 strong, with 20 machine-guns, pushed on to the Aqueduct bridge, crossed the Potomac, and advanced on Fort Myer from the north.

Another force of equal strength made for the Long Bridge, crossed, and approached the fort from the southeast.

Meanwhile the balance of the expedition as it reached the city took possession of the principal Government buildings. Five companies seized the Treasury; five companies the State, War, and Navy building; three companies took possession of the Capitol; and a detachment seized the Armory, capturing several machine-guns. Other detachments seized the banks, the Union Station, the Telephone Exchange, and the offices of the Postal Telegraph and Western Union. The balance of the troops, 1,000 strong, moved on the Washington Barracks.

Among the warnings sent out when Bron-

son, the war correspondent, crawled into
the Telephone Exchange, were two to the
garrisons at Fort Myer and Washington
Barracks.

At the former the force consisted of
400 cavalry and 400 field artillery with
several batteries of field-guns. The garrison
of Washington Barracks consisted of about
600 men. The commanders of each post
decided to unite their forces on the left
bank of the Potomac, and the Fort Myer
garrison at once moved out, a cavalry screen
being thrown forward to seize the Long
Bridge. About a mile from the bridge they
ran into a strong skirmish line of the second
German force, and fell back on their main
body, which hastily entrenched itself, the
field batteries moving to take up a position
to the rear. While the batteries were taking position, and before all the guns were
unlimbered, the first German force, which,
finding Fort Myer evacuated, had pushed

on with all speed, came up in the rear and opened a murderous machine-gun and rifle fire.

The cavalry wheeled and charged straight at the guns. Such was the impetus of their onrush, that those who survived that decimating fire, some 200 in all, broke through the first and second line before they were brought down. Those of the guns which could be brought into action swept the enemy with shrapnel at close range. Such an unequal contest could have but one issue. The gun detachments withered under the pitiless hail of German bullets, and when the enemy charged home, not a man was on his feet to dispute possession of the guns.

Leaving their own and the American wounded to be cared for by the stretcher-bearers of Fort Myer garrison, the Germans, now some 2,000 strong, mounted and moved back to the city. Here, on learn-

ing from dispatch riders that the force sent
to the Washington Barracks was heavily
engaged with the garrison in the neighbor-
hood of the steamboat wharves, they swung
around to the south and took the enemy on
the right flank and rear.

An hour later the Barracks and the Army
War College were captured, and by noon of
April 1st, the small American forces having been annihilated or captured, Washington passed into the hands of the Germans.

At dawn of the same day, the German
submarines, having passed in through the
Capes by night, sank or destroyed every
warship in the Norfolk yards, and at the
yards of the Newport News Shipbuilding
Company. Before the Germans had taken
possession of Washington, the news was
flashed from Philadelphia that a similar
submarine raid had resulted in the sinking
of the *South Carolina* and of the seven bat-

tleships in reserve and in ordinary, at the
League Island Yard, namely, the *Alabama,
Illinois, Kearsarge, Kentucky, Missouri,
Ohio,* and *Wisconsin.*

At noon, April 1st, the signal stations at
Cape Charles and Cape Henry reported
that a fleet of transports, flying the
German flag, was converging on the
entrance.

The rifle and mortar batteries at Fort
Monroe were instantly manned, and to the
amazement of all but the few who knew the
limitations of range, the fleet, in line ahead,
steamed boldly for that forbidden ground,
the main entrance to the Chesapeake, lying
to the south of the middle shoal. As the
fleet reached the entrance it slowed down,
and using the lead, crept in, hugging closely
the southerly edge of the shoal.

And then Fort Monroe spoke. From
her batteries there roared forth a salvo,
which, twenty seconds later, struck the

water 13,000 yards away, sending up huge
geysers of water. The projectiles, ricochet-
ting in great sweeping arcs, finally died
down into the water some thousands of
yards beyond.

Then came the mortar-battery salvo.
Lifting their stubby barrels to an angle of
45 degrees they shot their 12-inch shells
skyward. Several miles they rose, and just
one minute after the discharge four
columns of water rose about 1,000 yards
from the ships.

" I knew it," said the captain of the leading troopship, an officer of the German
naval reserve; " 18,000 yards is the extreme range of those bateries, and a study
of the chart convinced me that we could
just squeeze through."

And next day, April 3d, 5,000 German
infantry, together with the proper quota
of engineer corps, field batteries, signal and
medical corps, and the full equipment for a

force of 10,000 men, were landed below
Annapolis and moved on to Washington.

And on April 3d two events of the first
magnitude occurred: the President of the
United States announced that, acting on the
advice of his military advisers, he had directed that the seat of Government be
moved to Pittsburg; and to Pittsburg came
a proposal from Germany to cease all military operations, upon the agreement by the
United States to pay an indemnity of twelve
billion dollars, an advance payment of one
billion dollars in gold to be made on the day
the indemnity bond was signed.

XIV

SEEKING THE GERMAN FLEET

How it came about that I witnessed the greatest naval battle of all history from the fire-control platform of the flagship *Oklahoma* is readily explained. In the previous year I had offered for the consideration of the Navy Department a system of "director firing," which had been rejected on the ground that its mechanism was too delicate to stand the shock of battle.

The Department was developing a system of its own which gave great promise of success; and, in recognition of my interest in the subject, I had been invited to witness the final tests of the installation during the spring target practice of the *Oklahoma*.

There are moments in one's life which
stand out with sharp definition amid the
crowded and more or less blurred mem-
ories of the past. Among these I shall
ever reckon the breakfast hour, on the
morning of April 1st, in the wardroom of
the *Oklahoma,* flagship of the United
States North Atlantic fleet, which was at
anchor, on that particular day, off Vera
Cruz.

The Mexican situation had reached one
of its ever-recurring crises, with the result
that the army had moved down to the
Mexican border and the fleet to this Mexican port.

The conversation in the wardroom
mess had been drifting along in a desultory
way, when an orderly entered with a request for the presence of the executive officer in the Admiral's cabin. In a few minutes Commander Burnley returned, holding in his hand a wireless message. There

was that in his face which caused a sudden hush.

"I have here a radio message from Washington by way of Key West," he said, "which I will read: 'Germany has declared war on the United States. Have information German advance fleet is following southern course for Caribbean; second fleet on northern course for our Atlantic coast. Proceed full speed for Guantanamo Bay, Cuba, to take on coal and supplies. Find and destroy weaker advance German fleet. Send injured ships to Hampton Roads and proceed to Canal Zone, Panama. Under cover of guns of fortifications, await arrival of Third and Fourth Divisions of Atlantic fleet from Pacific, and proceed north in full strength to engage second fleet of enemy.'"

The tidings that war had been declared on the United States was flashed through the fleet, and a hurry call was sent ashore

for the return of the landing force of sea-
men and marines. Ships that were coaling
cast off their colliers, and before noon the
fleet had sailed.

Shortly before midnight of April 5th
the *Oklahoma* led the way into Guantanamo Bay, Cuba. The 6th was spent
in coaling, taking aboard full supplies of
stores and ammunition, and sending ashore
the boats and all superfluous ship's furniture. On the 7th, shortly before dawn,
the fleet, stripped for action, had sailed to
the eastward, to " find and destroy the
enemy."

Overnight, Admiral Willard, Commander-in-Chief of our fleet, had thrown out to
the eastward a strong scouting force—such
as it was—strong in numbers, but utterly
inadequate for its purpose. It consisted
of the three armored cruisers *Washington,
North Carolina,* and *Tennessee* and four
divisions of destroyers.

The cruisers were powerful ships carrying four 10-inch and sixteen 6-inch guns,
and they were capable of breaking through
any screen of the German light cruisers of
the *Karlsruhe* type; but they would be
utterly at the mercy of the 28-knot battle-
cruisers possessed by Germany, their best
speed being only a little over 22 knots.

The destroyers, twenty in all, should
never have been dispatched on such service.
Their place was with the main fleet. Had
the recommendations of the General
Board been followed, we would have possessed, on this disastrous day, a dozen 27-
knot scouts, and our main fleet, the first
line of defence of the United States against
invasion, would not have been left exposed
on both flanks to the destroyer attacks of
the enemy.

By the courtesy of the executive officer I
found myself on the forward fire-control
platform of the *Oklahoma*. As we cleared

the entrance to Guantanamo Bay and swung around to the eastward, from my station, 120 feet above the sea, I gazed with no little pride at the two divisions of dreadnoughts strung out astern, ship beyond ship at 500-yard intervals, in a stately column which covered some three miles of water.

Below me was the flagship, fresh from the builders' hands. Seen from above, she looked wonderfully like those deck-plan drawings which I had studied in the naval annuals. Forward was the new type of 3-gun turret, with its long, lean 14-inch guns looking for all the world like Brobdingnagian lead pencils. Abaft of it was turret No. 2, with its pair of guns reaching clear across the roof of turret No. 1. Astern I looked down into the yawning mouth of our huge single smokestack. Not so much as a wraith of tell-tale smoke drifted from its edge; merely the shimmer of heated gases—and I remembered that the boilers below were oil burners. Immediately abaft the mainmast, another pair of those beauties—the 14-inch—showed from No. 3 turret, with their muzzles poised a few feet above turret No. 4, from which protruded three 14's. Truly a noble ship, her powers of offence, represented by ten 14's and twenty-two 5's, being matched by the massive armor, 13½ to 18 inches in thickness, the like of which was to be found in no other navy of the world.

Five hundred yards astern, with a white feather of foam curling from her shapely stem, was the *Nevada*, twin sister to the flagship. Astern of her, at the same interval, were the *New York* and *Texas*, carrying each a battery of ten 14's and twenty-one 5's.

A wonderful piece, that 14—the pet and pride of the officers and men. Down at

Indian Head, it had passed its proving tests triumphantly. Fifty-four feet long, 63 tons in weight, it had fired its 1,400-pound shell with a velocity of 2,600 feet a second and an energy of 65,000 foot-tons. At a distance of 10,000 yards, the projectiles were capable of passing clean through 16 inches of Krupp armor. Elevated to its limit of 15 degrees, the gun could place a shell on a ship twelve miles distant.

And there were forty of these guns that could speak at once, and twice a minute each, in the first four ships of our line.

Astern of the *Texas*, I saw those stately ships, the *Arkansas* and *Wyoming,* mounting, each, twelve 12-inch guns in its six turrets, with a battery of twenty-one 5-inch rapid-firers to repel torpedo attack.

Seventh and eighth in line were the twin sisters, *Utah* and *Florida,* each carrying ten 12-inch guns and sixteen 5-inch. Last in the line were the *Delaware* and *North Dakota,* our earliest dreadnoughts, mounting ten 12's and fourteen 5's.

In displacement the ships varied from the 20,000 tons of the *Delaware* to the 27,500 tons of the *Oklahoma.* The belt armor was from 11 inches to 13½ inches in thickness, and the maximum speed of the fleet was 21 knots.

Every ship could fire its whole broadside on either beam, and in every minute of the coming engagement we would be able to hurl at the enemy 110 tons of projectiles, every one of which, if it landed squarely, would pass entirely through the belt armor of the enemy and burst in the interior of the ship.

Ship for ship and gun for gun, we knew that we could crush that German fleet, which, the radio had told us, was approaching somewhere to the eastward.

But where was the enemy? In what

strength was he? And, most important
question of all, how did he shoot?

Before that sun, which I noted was just
showing the golden edge of his rim above
the horizon, had set, those questions had
received their answer amid the fruitless
heroism, the cataclysmic destruction, of
the greatest sea fight in naval history.

XV

THE BATTLE OF THE CARIBBEAN

I REMEMBER it was while six bells were striking that there came the following radio call from one of our scouts, the armored cruiser *Washington:* "Approaching St. Nicholas," it said, "fog lifted, disclosing screen of five battle-cruisers of the enemy, steaming abreast, distance 20,000 yards, covering a column of ten ships, apparently battleships. All are heading west. Am returning full speed, 22½ knots." At 7:15 A.M. came another message: "Enemy, in chase, has opened fire at 18,000 yards and is coming up fast." And then the story came in quick sequence. At 7:30: "Enemy at 15,000 yards is using forward 12- and 11-inch guns on all five ships. Am replying with two after 10-

inch." At 7:40: "Received two shells,
raking starboard battery." At 7:45:
"Shell in boiler-room and two funnels
gone. Speed 15 knots." At 7:55: "Steering gear gone—after turret disabled—
heavy casualties—am shot to pieces—going down by stern, colors flying—sorry
cannot give details battleship fleet—our
position is lat.——!"

A wireless call was sent for our destroyers to rejoin the fleet at full speed,
and the speed of the fleet was raised to
17 knots.

And then we saw them—on the starboard bow. First the masts, with the flut-
ter of the battle-flags discernible; then
the smokestacks, the turrets, the hulls, and,
yes! the five battle-cruisers, which only a
brief hour before had sent the *Washington*
with her gallant company to the bottom.

And then, up over the horizon, sil-
houetted sharply against the eastern sky,

there came, a mile or more astern, the van
of the battleship line—one—two—three—
eight in all: the German dreadnoughts.
And now the battle-cruisers began to swing
around, at full speed, in a wide turn to
port, following in the wake of their flagship, *Derfflinger,* until they had made a
turn of 16 points, and were heading to the
east. Simultaneously, each ship of the
two battleship divisions swung around,
with helm hard over, until it had turned
16 points. When the maneuver was completed, the Germans were heading east in
two parallel columns, the battleship column abreast of us at a distance of 16,000
yards, and the battle-cruisers some 5,000
yards off their starboard bow and 21,000
yards from our line.

In order to secure more of an offing
from the Cuban coast, and obtain ample
room for maneuvering, our Admiral signaled for every ship to turn four points

to starboard; a maneuver which was instantly followed by the Germans.

" Ha, ha," laughed an ensign, who, with
his eye at the range-finder, was calling the
distances into a telephone mouthpiece,
" they don't want to come too close to our
14-inch guns; and as for the battle-cruisers,
they are going to stay out of the scrap al-
together; for at over 20,000 yards their
11's can never reach us."

" You are wrong there," said Lieutenant Carlisle, the spotter; " the German
batteries can elevate to 30 degrees, which
is just twice as much as we can. Their
11's have the advantage in range, carrying
up to 26,000 yards, as a matter of fact.
See that? They are trying a ranging shot
at 21,000 yards."

And, sure enough, there was a flash
from the forward turret of the *Derfflinger,* and thirty-five seconds later, with
a deep moaning roar, a shell passed over

our heads and dropped into the sea, five
hundred yards beyond the ship.

And now Admiral Willard, having obtained sufficient offing, brought his fleet
back into column again, ready for the great
trial of strength.

There was another flash from the *Derfflinger,* and half a minute later the shell
struck 300 yards to starboard of the *Oklahoma.*

" Good shooting," said the ensign,
" now for the salvo."

But it did not come—not yet. Instead,
the leading ship of the German dreadnought column tried for range. The shell
struck 400 yards short. The next was 600
yards over. And then came the salvos.
From both ships there burst a flash of
flame, from the battle-cruiser first and, a
few seconds later, from the dreadnought
—and the *Oklahoma* was the target of
each.

With a crash that seemed to rend the heavens, those twenty 12-inch shells "straddled" our ship, one making a square hit on our belt and the others striking the sea on either beam, and sending up vast columns of water that rose some 250 feet in the air, and fell like broken waterspouts upon our decks. We on the fire-control platform were drenched and found ourselves standing over our boot-tops in water.

But what of the *Oklahoma?* Had her guns been silent? Far from it.

As soon as the German columns straightened out after their turn to the eastward, Ensign Brown at the range-finder began to telephone the range to the fire-control station below decks. "Sixteen thousand five hundred yards; 16,200; 16,-000; 15,500; 15,000." And looking over the rail, I noted that the center gun in No. 1 turret was lifting its muzzle. Then came

a snapping crash, a burst of flame, a drift
of light-brown smoke, and the 1,400-
pound shell was away on its flight.
Twenty seconds later a beautiful snow-
white column rose a little short of the German flagship and slightly astern. The
" spotter," his eyes glued to his glasses,
called into the mouthpiece of his telephone:
" Up 300; left 6."

Down to the central station below the
water-line went the message. The necessary corrections in the elevation of the
gun were there figured out and telephoned
to the sight-setter at the gun. Again a
shell sped to the mark. This time the
splash was beyond the ship and ahead.
" Down 200; right 3," called the spotter.
And now the necessary corrections being
made on every gun in the ship's battery,
the fire-control officer, holding the cross-
hairs of his telescope on the German flagship, pressed a button and all the 14-inch

guns in our battery let go together, and the ten 1,400-pound shells soared into the heavens, visible for a few seconds to the eye. There was a magnificent burst of water at the German flagship, and, as it fell away, through my glasses I could see that her after smokestack was gone. The ragged outline of her deck, moreover, showed where the shells had burst inboard, lifting the deck, and apparently jamming the after turret.

And when the flagship had spoken, every ship down our line burst forth in flame and fury. The Germans fired with greater frequency and the storm of their shells, striking the water, raised such a mass of broken spray that, at times, I could see no farther than the second ship astern.

The American ships fired with greater deliberation, and, evidently, with greater accuracy. Moreover, against a com-

bined broadside for the enemy dreadnoughts of thirty-two 12's and thirty-two
11's, we opposed a total broadside of
forty 14's and sixty-four 12's. The fire
of the German battle-cruisers at 20,000
yards was too inaccurate to be much more
than annoying, although some deck hits
were made.

After ten minutes of furious fighting,
superior weight of metal began to tell.
The flagship *Thuringen,* with one smokestack gone and the after turret out of
action, began to slow down; finally dropping to the rear, leaving the *Helgoland*
to lead the line. Later, she picked up and
took station at the rear of the German
column. Then the *Oldenburg,* second in
line, took a sudden shear, and began to
circle, finally coming back on her own line
and cutting in between the *Thuringen*
(last in line) and the *Posen.* A 14-inch
shell striking fair on the conning tower

had wrecked it and jammed her steering wheel. Ultimately, she straightened out, 1,500 yards astern of the column, which slowed down to cover her until she closed up.

The first ship to be put out of action was the *Nassau,* which succumbed to the concentrated salvos of the four leading ships of our line. Under the impact of their 14-inch shells, it looked through our glasses as though a whole section of her side armor was driven bodily into the ship. She dropped out of line mortally hurt, and, heeling rapidly, capsized and sank, fifteen minutes after the action opened.

Our leading ships then concentrated on the *Helgoland* and *Ostfriesland,* first and second in line; and in order to cover them the battle-cruisers, risking the penetration of their belts by our 14's, drew ahead clear of the dreadnought line and closing in to

15,000 yards began to plant their salvos on the *Oklahoma* and *Nevada.*

Their shells, falling at a steep angle, were dropping on our decks; and it was one of these that pierced the protective deck of the *Nevada,* smashed her low pressure turbines, and threw this fine ship out of the line. She stopped and drifted astern. When I last saw her, she was blazing away with her 5-inch batteries at a swarm of German destroyers, which had rushed in, like a crowd of angry terriers, to get her with the torpedo.

The fight had now been on for half an hour and we were asserting our superiority. The battle-cruiser *Von der Tann* had been badly hit and was settling by the stern. The fire from the German dreadnoughts had perceptibly slackened, and the *Thuringen,* at the tail of the column, was again in trouble with her steering-gear and had fallen behind. Although our ships had been badly knocked about in their upper works and some of the turrets had been disabled, the water line was intact on every ship. Victory was in sight, and we on the fire-control platform were jubilantly slapping each other on the back, when, happening to look landwards (we were now clearing Cape Maysi, the extreme easterly point of Cuba), I saw the leading ships of a column of warships moving past the point and bearing down diagonally upon our port bow.

I touched the spotter on the shoulder: " Carlisle, look at that; what is it? "

He swung his glasses upon the fleet (it was clear of the point by now). " That, my dear sir, is the other and stronger half of the German fleet, four *Koenigs* and the five *Kaisers*."

" Good Heavens! Then we are in for it."

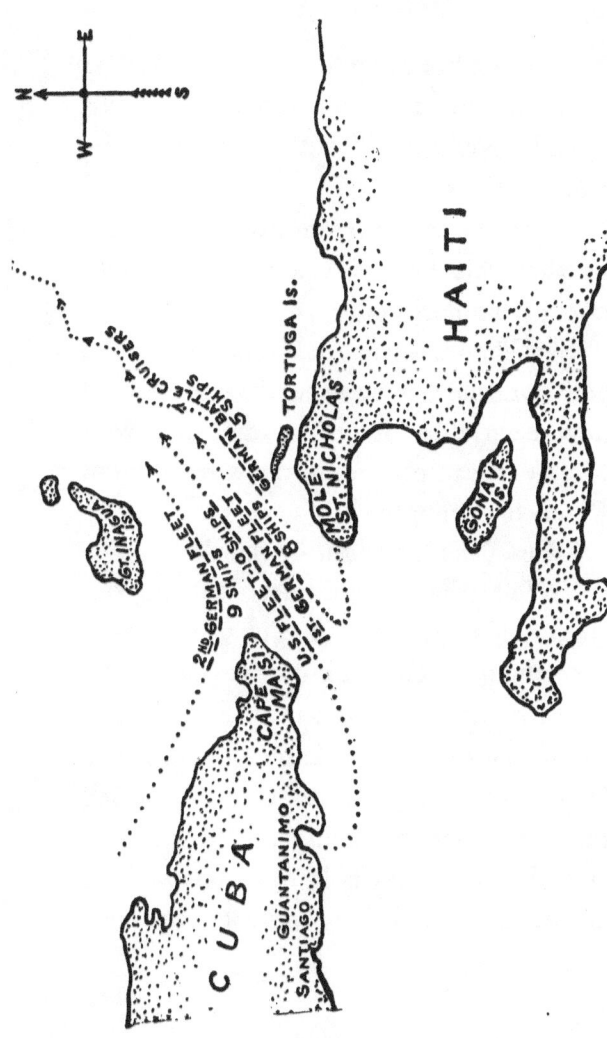

SKETCH (NOT TO SCALE) SHOWING RELATIVE POSITION OF THE FLEETS IN THE BATTLE OF
THE CARIBBEAN.

"In for a licking," my dear boy, "if they can do as good shooting as our friends over there," with a wave of the hand to the starboard.

"But the radio from Key West told us that this fleet was a thousand miles north from here."

Carlisle was silent for a moment. "Did you not think it strange that we should have been able to communicate only with Key West radio station—not a word from Colon or Arlington?"

"Yes, I had thought of that."

"Well, that second fleet coming out from under the lee of Cuba has made everything as clear as day to me. The Germans have raided our coasts (why,— we may never live to know), seized Key West, and, using our secret code (which their confounded Intelligence Service has undoubtedly gotten hold of), have led us, in their own good time, and with true Ger-

man precision, into this trap. Just look at
that! They are going to tee us."

And there we saw the four battle-
cruisers, going 28 knots, forge ahead of
the German column, and draw in, diagonally, across our path.

By the time the second fleet of the
enemy had closed in to 12,000 yards and
opened fire, the cruiser division was zig-
zagging across our course, 10,000 yards
ahead, and delivering a raking fire right
down our line, first letting fly to starboard,
then to port.

A hurricane of fire and steel smote the
head of the American line. By precon-
certed plan, every ship of the enemy, from
starboard, from port, and from dead
ahead, concentrated on the *Oklahoma*.
Never had such a fury of shells stormed
upon ship or fortress as found and
searched out the American flagship. In
those brief minutes before she sank, all

semblance of a ship had gone out of her. The roar of bursting shells was continuous. From side to side and from end to end they tore through her quivering frame and laughed at her dying agony.

And I am told that what happened to her happened at the head of the surviving line, until the last ship had gone,—the column melting away before that concentrated fire like a bar of sealing wax before a blowpipe.

I remember, as the noble ship keeled swiftly over, how the fire-control platform described a mighty arc through the air, and flung us into the shell-lashed waters. My last recollection of that holocaust is of seeing the *Arkansas,* flashing from stem to stern with the burst of high-explosive shell as she swept by. Then a shell fragment grazed my head.

.   .   .   .

The water, or I know not what, brought

me to. Far in the distance the flash and
smoke and roar of battle marked where
the last American ship was being done to
death, the dear old flag flaunting its "no
surrender" message to the bitter end.
And then, as the sad vision and all vision
began to fade away, I heard sharp words
of command, and the swish of backing pro-
pellers, and something jerked me violently
by the collar, and I was lying upon my
back, and a familiar voice was saying:
"Bless my soul, if it isn't Watson! What
in the name of the unexpected and impossible are *you* doing here?"

And I had been fished out of the water
by a boat hook and landed on the deck of
the U. S. destroyer *Patterson;* and there
was Commander Judson, whose guest I had
been on this very boat, during a never-to-
be-forgotten week of the summer maneuvers last year.

"I came down to witness director firing

on the *Oklahoma* and—well—I saw it.—
And you, what are you going to do?"

" Beat it for Hampton Roads, or any
other point where I can get in to tell the
good people of the United States, and their
good representatives in the halls of Congress, to what a pretty mess they have
brought their navy, as the result of
interference, parsimony, and neglect!"

XVI

REAPING THE WHIRLWIND

THE plan of campaign for the invasion of the United States, as formulated by the Great General Staff at Berlin, comprised three major operations:

I. To make a surprise attack upon the coast by a raiding force, and capture Washington and the principal seaboard cities, harbors, and naval bases.

II. To destroy the enemy fleet and obtain command of the sea.

III. By the instant seizure of all the arsenals, gun factories, and powder works, to prevent the development of the great potential strength of the United States in men capable of bearing arms.

So perfect was the preparation of Germany; so complete the unpreparedness of the great country against which she launched her attack, that within a week of the declaration of war her fleet had sunk the enemy and was in undisputed command of the sea, and her army had captured the National Capital and the two leading seaports of the country.

.   .   .   .

At the very hour when the Mayor of New York received the ultimatum of Admiral Buchner, there dropped anchor in the Narrows the new 54,000-ton liner *Bismarck*. It was her maiden voyage (duly advertised), and she had on board 10,000 German troops with their full equipment. The next day she was joined by the *Imperator* and the *Vaterland,* and as soon as the signal " cease firing " had been made from the *Koenig,* the three great ships, carrying 30,000 troops, or as many as the total regular mobile army in the United States at that hour, steamed to

the Hoboken and Chelsea docks and began
the work of debarkation. Before night on
April 2d, the German forces in New York,
including the garrisons at the forts, numbered 35,000 men.

To Boston came the *Cecilie,* the *Kaiser
Wilhelm II,* and many another well-
remembered liner, crowded with men and
equipment. Night and day the soldiers
of the Kaiser poured down the gangways
of the ships, formed in column, marched
from the docks to the armories, and were
billeted throughout the cities.

And now, the need for secrecy being
removed, transports steamed boldly up
the Chesapeake, and Washington received its quota of the first reënforcements
from Germany. Here, the guns, horses,
transport wagons, etc., were placed on
pontoons for transport from ship to landing beach.

So excellent were the facilities for de-

barkation afforded by the possession of
New York and Boston, that by April 5th,
including the raiding force, two army
corps, or 80,000 troops, fully equipped and
ready for service in the field, had been
landed in America.

And thereafter during the next five days,
the faster ships of the transports which
sailed from Germany on April 1st began
to arrive, warping into the piers at New
York and Boston, which had been vacated
by the earlier transports; so that by April
10th the German forces in the United
States had been raised to 100,000 men.

Bold, indeed, was the strategy which
dared to send this army to sea in unarmed
transports, while the main fleet of the
enemy was still " in being," or intact upon
the high seas. Had not the great Mahan
and many another authority before him
laid it down, that before troops were embarked the enemy fleet must be either

sunk or securely blockaded in its own
ports? True; but, "Other times, other
customs." The advent of the seagoing
submarine and of the wireless had intro-
duced factors which had upset the old
formulas of war.

The possession by the enemy of a force
of seagoing submarines enabled them, at
one stroke, to clear the coasts of every hostile ship from Canada to the Panama
Canal; and the capture of the radio plants
and the possession by Germany of the
U. S. Navy Secret Code made it possible
to lure its main fleet into a position where
it could be overwhelmed by superior numbers.

Finally, on April 11th there appeared
off the American coast a great fleet of 45
transports, having on board 100,000
troops, and convoyed by the pre-dreadnought ships of the *Deutschland* and
Wittlesbach classes. It divided, the five

Deutschlands convoying half of the force
to New York and the five *Wittlesbachs*
proceeding with the other half to the Delaware.   The defences of the Delaware
having been already taken from the land
side, the fleet steamed up to Philadelphia.

By the 14th of April, or just two weeks
after the declaration of war, an army of
200,000 of the picked veterans of the recent European conflict had been landed
on American shores and was prepared to
move into the interior for the subjugation
of the country.

.   .   .   .

And that was how it came about that
the United States—the wealthiest and, po-
tentially in its undeveloped wealth of men
and natural resources, the most powerful
country on earth—found itself, in the
space of two eventful weeks, held fast in
the " mailed fist " of a foreign foe.

Having, lo! these many years, " sown to
the wind " the seeds of pacificist delusion,
of political self-seeking, of amazing self-
sufficiency, and of fatuous neglect, she was
now to " reap the whirlwind " of disillu-
sionment and humiliation in a profound
national disaster!

.   .   .   .

To describe in any detail the sequence
of the operations by which the German
Commander-in-Chief, within two weeks of
the opening of hostilities had captured all
the arsenals, and arms and powder works
lying between the coast and the Alleghanies, would take a volume in itself.
That must be the work of the future his-
torian. It will suffice for the present
purpose to sketch the mere outline of those
tragic events which came to be known
thereafter as The Great American Dé-
bacle!

Immediately upon the capture of Bos-

ton, New York, and Washington, detachments were told off to seize the railway
yards and terminals, and to commandeer
such automobiles and motor trucks as
were best adapted to army transport.
This was done in each case on April 1st,
and early on the same day strong flying
detachments, with numerous batteries of
machine-guns, were rushed out by rail and
by automobile to seize the bridges and
tunnels on the main lines of the New
Haven, the New York Central, and the
Pennsylvania systems. Every few hours
additional reënforcements were pushed
forward to strengthen and hold these
strategic points, until the several armies
of occupation could be brought up from
the coast by rail.

And on April 6th, the railroads being
securely held, the main advance began.

From Boston a force of 5,000 men was
thrown into Portsmouth, and three regi-

ments, comprising about 10,000 men, moved down the coast, capturing the Fore River Shipbuilding plant at Quincy, Mass., where most of the United States submarines are built, and seizing the Torpedo Station at Newport, R. I., the submarine engine works at Groton, and the port of New London.

By way of the New Haven four-track road, 15,000 troops moved from New York into Connecticut, capturing, in succession, Bridgeport, New Haven, Hartford, and Springfield, Mass. This placed in possession of the enemy such important works as those of the Union Metallic Cartridge Company, the American & British Mfg. Co. for making field-guns, the Winchester and Marlin works, the Colt works, and, greatest disaster of all, the United States Aresnal, where the rifles for the Regular Army and the Organized Militia are made.

The army of invasion by way of the Hudson River, 15,000 strong, moving by the four-track road of the New York Central, captured Iona Island, an important shell and powder depot of the U. S. Navy, and at Troy, N. Y., took possession of the Government works for the manufacture of heavy coast-defence guns and mortars. Pushing on they soon had possession, at Utica and Ilion, of the Remington and of the Savage Small Arms works.

The invasion of New Jersey was effected by a division (20,000 men). Strong detachments of this force seized the United States Army Arsenal and Powder works near Dover, and the Powder works of the Du Pont Powder Company at Parlin, Pompton Lakes, and other New Jersey points. Another detachment moved through Easton and took possession of the Bethlehem Steel Works, one of the most important gun and armor plants in the

world. The balance of the force, comprising some 15,000 men, seized Philadelphia, and took over the great shipbuilding yards of the Cramps at Philadelphia
and of the New York Shipbuilding Company at Camden, N. J. Following this,
the Germans moved down on both sides
of the Delaware and captured, from the
land side, the fortifications on the river
guarding the approaches to Philadelphia.

From Washington 7,000 troops moved
on Baltimore, and pushing on, occupied
Wilmington and the great powder works
of the Du Pont Powder Company at Car-
ney Point. Fort Monroe was reduced by
bombardment, from a point beyond the
range of its guns, by the battleship fleet
which convoyed the second half of the
German Army; and when this had been accomplished, the Norfolk Navy Yard and
the Newport News Shipyard were cap-

tured by a force of 3,000 men from Washington.

And thus, by April 10th, the major
naval and military operations of the German plan of invasion had been completed.
The United States main fleet was sunk,
Washington and the principal seacoast
cities were captured, and the arsenals and
gun factories (with the exception of that at
Rock Island) for arming and supplying any
new armies which might be raised were in
German hands.

Eight billions of the twenty billions
which was the ultimate object of the invasion had been pledged. It now remained
to secure from the Federal Government
the twelve billion dollars, which had been
demanded as the price of peace and the
evacuation of United States territory.

.   .   .   .

Let it not be for one moment supposed
that while its territory was thus being out-

raged and overrun, the United States was
tamely submissive.   The regular army,
alas! except for the slender garrisons, was
concentrated thousands of miles away on
the Mexican border; but the moment the
news of the invasion was flashed inland,
orders were given for the mobilization of
the militia and every emergency measure
was taken to meet the invader.

But so quickly did he strike inland that
it was at once evident that any concentration of troops in the East, in sufficient
strength for effectual resistance, was impossible.   Therefore, acting on the advice
of his Chief of Staff, the President sent
out an order for the retirement of all
forces, regular and militia, behind the
general line of the Alleghanies, and their
concentration at Pittsburg, the temporary
seat of Government.

And so, with smothered rage, the de-
scendants of the men who fought at Lex-

ington, Bunker Hill, and Yorktown saw
the richest and most populous section of
their country handed over for occupation
by a foreign army; and the bitterness of
that hour was not assuaged by the thought
that this evacuation by the scattered American
can troops was the only alternative to their
capture or absolute annihilation by the perfectly
organized army of occupation, back
of which, thanks to the absolute command
of the sea, lay the millions of the Kaiser's
army.

Bitter as gall, too, was the thought that,
if the country had listened to the oft-repeated
warnings of its military advisers,
the enemy could never have landed on
American soil, or, having done so, would
have been met by a quick concentration in
such superior strength as to drive him back
to his ships.

XVII

THE CAPTURE OF PITTSBURG—AND PEACE

No answer having been received by the Commander-in-Chief of the German forces in America to the proposals forwarded to the United States Government at Pittsburg, orders were given in Berlin on April 3d for the immediate embarkation of a third army of 100,000 men for the seat of war. Also, instructions were forwarded to New York to move in full strength on Pittsburg.

Forthwith, an army of 150,000 men began to concentrate at Philadelphia—50,000 men being considered amply sufficient to hold the cities already captured. This confidence was based on the absolutely reliable data furnished to Berlin before the war by the German Intelligence Service

as to the total effectives (90,000 regular
and militia) in the country, and on the information furnished from the same source
as to the complete evacuation of the Atlantic States by the United States military
forces and their concentration at Pittsburg.

Before the movement of troops dis-
closed the plan of campaign, strong advance forces were thrown forward to hold
the bridges on the line of the Pennsylvania
Railroad across the Alleghanies. The
main force moved forward on April 16th
by rail and motor car, on parallel roads,
until it was halted at the great stone bridge
of the Pennsylvania Railroad across the
Susquehanna, near Harrisburg, three
arches of which had been blown up by the
United States Army Engineers. The Germans ultimately crossed by temporary tres-
tle bridging, and by a pontoon bridge,
which they threw across the river. Sharp

fighting occurred between the American
rear guard and the advance screen of the
German Army at every point up the Juniata
Valley that offered strong positions for
defence.   On April 20th and 21st one of
the most glorious feats of arms in American history was performed, when a united
force of 10,000 regulars and 15,000 militia held the pass at the summit of the Alleghanies for two days, throwing back the
van of the German advance, and being finally dislodged only when massed batteries
of 400 guns caused them to retreat—the
whole force getting away down the Cone-
maugh Valley with their artillery and
wounded.

The American Army, consisting of
28,000 regulars and 42,000 effectives of
the militia, with 30,000 partially trained
and ill-equipped militia in reserve, had
taken position for the defence of Pittsburg on the historic field of Braddock's

defeat. The little army was strongly entrenched; but in field artillery it was sadly
deficient, having only 180 field-guns,
where it should have had 350. There
was a similar shortage in machine-gun
batteries.

Against the Americans was deployed an
army which, in spite of the engagements in
crossing the mountains, still numbered
145,000 men of all arms. It was completely equipped, and of the 7.7 centimeter
field-gun it possessed over 850, besides several batteries of 8.2-inch field howitzers.

It is not within the scope of this narra-
tive to attempt any description of the Battle of Braddock. Thanks to the skill with
which the American position was chosen,
the admirable advantage that was taken
of the terrain in laying out the trenches
and emplacing the batteries, and above all
the matchless courage and endurance with
which the American Army clung to its

position—the onset of the German invasion was checked and its first rush broken and thrown back in confusion upon the main body. Only after two days of the bloodiest charge and countercharge, and when the whole mass of the German artillery had blasted the American trenches out of all semblance of earthworks, did the remnant of the American forces fall back on Pittsburg. After destroying all the bridges the army fell back to take up a strong defensive position along the west bank of the Ohio.

The seat of government was transferred to Cincinnati; and, within a few days, an emissary arrived from the German Commander-in-Chief, with the proposal that, on the condition of the payment by the Federal Government of twelve billion dollars and its abandonment of the " Monroe Doctrine," the German Army would be reëmbarked, leaving sufficient forces to

hold the principal custom-houses on the Atlantic and Gulf Coast until the indemnity
was paid.

A council of war was called by the President for the purpose of discussing the military situation.   Present were the Cabinet,
the Chief of Staff of the Army, and the
President of the General Board of the
Navy.

The President of the United States,
whose poise, so far as any outward indica-
tions might show, seemed to have been in
no wise disturbed by the stupendous
calamity which had overtaken the country,
said:

" The question as to whether it will be
the part of wisdom to accept the conditions
of the enemy, or carry on the war until he
is crushed and driven back to the sea, is a
naval and military one.   There are two
questions, indeed, to be answered: Is there
any possibility of our defeating the enemy

fleet and cutting off the German Army
from its base; and failing that, what are
the prospects of our raising an army or
armies of sufficient strength to defeat the
land forces of the enemy and drive him
back to the sea."

"So far as the naval situation is concerned," said the President of the General
Board, "the case is hopeless. It became
so on the fatal day when every dreadnought possessed by the American Navy
was sunk in the Caribbean. For, although,
in spite of the great odds against which we
fought (10 ships against 22), eight of the
enemy were sunk, they still have 14 ships
of the dreadnought class off our coast, besides 10 ships of the pre-dreadnought
class, to say nothing of strong divisions
and flotillas of cruisers, destroyers, and
submarines. Our own pre-dreadnought
fleet is in the Pacific, and, because of the
preponderance of the enemy in the At-

lantic, it must remain there. We cannot
increase our naval strength; for all of our
navy yards and shipbuilding plants on the
Atlantic seaboard are in the hands of the
enemy. Whatever the duration of the war,
Mr. President, the command of the sea
will remain with the Germans; and they
will be free to bring over the whole
German Army, should they wish to do
so."

He was followed by the Chief of Staff,
who said:

" As to the military situation, Mr. President, the conditions are easily stated.

" The enemy is in undisputed possession
of the richest, most valuable, and most
densely populated section of the United
States. He holds all that part of the
country north of the Potomac lying between the Alleghanies and the Atlantic
Coast. Being in command of the sea and
possessing ample transport, he is free to

land on our shores as many troops as he
may desire. His army can live off the
land. Having possession of the principal
ports of the country, he can collect those
revenues which have formed the greater
half of the revenues of the Federal Government; and our Treasury will be de-
pleted to just that extent. Therefore, if
we carry on the war, the cost of the war,
not merely to us but to the enemy, must
be borne by the United States.

"The question of our ability to raise
and equip an army sufficient in numbers,
equipment, and training to enable us to
drive the enemy back to the sea depends,
primarily, upon the strength of the forces
which he may bring over. So great is the
prize for which Germany would contend
that she would match corps with corps,
army with army; and, supposing that no
European complications arise, it is conceiv-
able that we should find ourselves con-

fronted by the full strength of the German Army or, say, including the first and second reserves, by 4,000,000 men."

Here the Secretary of State interposed to say:

"The President has only to send out a call for volunteers, and out of our 100,-000,000 citizens, 10,000,000 would spring to arms before the sun had set."

"True, Mr. Secretary," said the Chief of Staff, "but you must remember that securing the men is the simplest part of the problem. Moreover, you must not forget that the most populous portion of the country is held by the enemy, and if he can prevent it—which he will—not a single volunteer will be available from the captured territory.

"The problem, however, is not to get the men, but the officers to lead them and the rifles, uniforms, ammunition, and above all the artillery, with which to equip them. Without these, your 10,000,000 men, Mr. Secretary, as I told you in Washington, would be merely a mob, 10,000,-000 strong.

" Take the question of artillery alone. Without it, to send an army to battle with the superbly equipped German troops would be to send the brave fellows to certain slaughter. To equip an army of 4,000,000 men with field artillery alone would call for 20,000 3-inch guns; and the equipment with howitzers and machineguns, to say nothing of rifles and ammunition of all kinds, would be on the same scale.

" Where are we going to obtain all this *matériel?* Practically all the arsenals, depots, gunshops, rifle factories, and powder works of the United States lie in that part of the country which is held by the enemy.

"So the question of how long it would

take us to drive out the Germans is one not
of patriotism but of mechanics. If I could
tell you, offhand, Mr. President, how long
it would take to build, equip, and man the
factories necessary to manufacture the
rifles, field-guns, powder, uniforms, and
tentage for an army of one million, or two,
three, or four million men, as the case
might be, I could tell you how long
it would be before we were ready
to drive the enemy from our lost territory.

"At a rough guess, I should say that it
would be not less than two and a half
years, and if he developed his full military
strength, it might be five or six."

The Chief of Staff paused, swept his
glance over the Cabinet, and resumed:

"If I may be allowed to state what
seems to me to be the wise course, the truly
patriotic course, in this crisis——"

"Certainly," said the President.

" I would suggest that the Government pay this indemnity, and write it off on the National Ledger as the cost of being taught the great national duty of military preparedness."

THE END.